We Are Still Breathing

Dianah Ose Aigiomawu

To my husband, Hazel Eyez
No one will ever understand, but us.
My kids, Danny and Sophia - you give joy a whole
new meaning.

Contents

Twist of Fate 6

Mazino Hall 19

Still Breathing 32

The New Benin Market 49

When Love Is Not Enough 63

Diary of a Wedding Planner 77

The Applicant 99

In a Gilded Cage 118

The Passenger 134

The Boy in the Garden 145

    Acknowledgements 151

Editor's Note 153

Twist of Fate

When suffering knocks at your door and you say there is no seat for him, he tells you not to worry because he has brought his own stool.

-Chinua Achebe

The Ighalos lived a few houses away from us, in the poshest part of our not so posh neighbourhood. People talked about them in hushed tones these days since Oare their oldest daughter travelled to Italy. The truth is, they always talked about them in hushed tones, even when they lived in the poorest parts of the Estate close to Iwogban.

They were a family of fourteen, though it was once rumoured that there were thirty of them living in the one bedroom apartment, but then we were kids, and exactitude was not our forte.

The Ighalo kids all looked alike, and always seemed to be in small groups of same aged children. Dark skinned, so dark they reminded me of the caricatures on the popular French text, *France Afrique*. I sometimes wondered if the Ighalos had multiple sets of twins and triplets, or if they were just poorly spaced.

Some houses in the low income Federal Housing Estate, Ikpoba hill were certainly lower than the name implied. Maybe in the *80s* when the government built them, they might have been worth something but now they looked like a uniformed slum. White paint dating back to the *80s*, buildings all rundown, and the famous red soil in Benin make the houses look even dirtier.

The lower part of the walls where the flood had ravaged the semi-detached flats left most of the un-renovated houses with just the ashy coloured plastering and old brownish green moss. Most of the buildings were still standing only because back then, foundations were solid and well-laid.

7

Mr. Ighalo had somehow managed to secure a mortgage on one of the single roomed apartments back in the *80s*. He neither renovated nor extended the building. In all fairness to him, as a retired driver in the ministry of works, with a fish seller for a wife who was pregnant every other year, there was never enough for the family. Neither could they have saved up anything.

Mr Ighalo was very tall, thin and walked with his back hunched. I am almost certain he was not always so. Not easy for me to visualize, but I guess he was once straight backed, maybe not so lanky-that was all probably before the kids came.

Now all he did was drink *ogogoro*, the local gin at Mama Efe's, the beer parlour at Street 21. It was rumoured that Mama Efe and her daughters sold more than just beer and the illicit gin. But that's a story for another day.

"Omoye!"

I knew why my mum was calling even before I ran towards the kitchen. I had left the pot of *om'ebe* on the two burner gas cooker, and I could smell it burning as I got closer.

"You left the soup on the fire to go and gossip, *abi*?"

She held the soup spoon menacingly in front of her. I was scared she would throw it at me as my eyes darted to the nearest exit.

"*Nene*, I went to put the rag out in the sun. Then I saw that pigeons were eating the melon seeds you spread in the sun. I had to drive them away…" I lied with so much ease, I was ashamed of myself.

8

Nene is the Ishan word for mum. We barely spoke the language, so it always seemed to soften my mum's heart whenever I called her that. It worked though. Mum's hands came down when she heard I had saved her precious melon seeds.

"So it took you the whole day to do that?" She continued in a less angry tone.

I knew she would not give in that easily. I quickly apologized and she stormed out of the kitchen still angry, especially as the black soup I had almost ruined was being made for my uncle, Osagie.

Black soup, as the name implied, was not actually black but a dark greenish soup. It was a delicacy peculiar to the Ishan-speaking people of Edo State. Leafy green vegetables are blended into a green mushy paste and cooked in palm oil with fish, meat and lots of crayfish.

It looked rather murky to the uninitiated but amazingly delicious when eaten with *fufu* or pounded yam.

Uncle Osagie lived in Spain and usually requested for traditional meals whenever he visited. Black soup or *om'ebe* was certainly one of his favourites.

I had gone out to spread the wet rag like I told Nene, then I heard Mr. Ighalo singing:

> *No go sawa, no dey ever sawa*
> *Ogogoro no dey sawa o*

I knew it wasn't right to make fun of the drunken man, but I could at least peep over the fence. If I was lucky, he would probably dance for a while or, for better fun, trip while trying to do the dance.

Other kids were out there, watching, cheering him on but all I could do was look over the fence, as my mum would skin us alive if she ever caught us outside our old black gate.

I have nothing against the Ighalos, true that the kids were always very dirty and troublesome, which made it very difficult for anyone to feel sorry for them in their malnourished, poverty-stricken state.

Their mum, Mrs Ighalo was a very cantankerous woman who was just as mean as she was dirty. We heard tales of how the fishes she smoked for sale at the local Oregbeni Market every five days were usually stored in the toilet corridor, as their house was small and had no space. It made sense then considering the number of people in the house and the space available to them.

Mum had forbidden us from buying fish from them. In her words "The neighborhood is dirty enough without us fishing from the Ighalos' toilet." We had all laughed and joked about the clueless buyers at the market.

My younger brother, Ehis, had jokingly pointed out one day: "Mummy, you have no idea where your customer at the market stores hers either."

"I don't know," Mum said defensively, "but I am sure she doesn't store them in her toilet," she added.

From the slight furrow on her forehead, I could tell she was pondering the same thing now that Ehis mentioned it. I was right. Mum did not buy any smoked fish at the next market day. She muttered something about smoked fish not being healthy because of the smoke, and that fresh fish would suffice henceforth. I knew better than argue. We all knew why but accepted her flimsy attempt at an explanation.

I am not certain if Oare was actually the Ighalos' firstborn or just the oldest female child but when she made money, she was certainly treated like the oldest.

Oare disappeared for months and we all assumed she had been sent away to live with a relative in the village. Her dad had threatened to send her to the village when she got pregnant sometime last year. We never saw her tummy protruding. We did not see a baby. Yet, she was always seen in dark street corners with the boys in the neighbourhood.

Things were really rough for the Ighalos. The younger kids all looked malnourished. The older boys were always suspected to be in the gang of other neighbourhood boys who stole people's clothes from the lines or chickens from the coops and carried out petty burglaries. These were not rumours, as one or two of the older boys had been caught and arrested by the small local police station on Street 32.

The Ighalos had lost a lot too. The youngest boy had died of malnutrition. Another had been carried off by the flood at a badly-eroded road. These losses had both happened within a single year.

The Ighalos' kids could not register for any terminal exam and none attempted a higher institution till Oare travelled to Italy. Theirs was a life filled with overwhelming poverty, suffering and despair. But they were resilient. Some of the boys worked at sites for some cash and tended a farm from where they harvested cassava and made *garri* for sale sometimes. But with so many mouths to feed, they could barely survive from these little earnings. But all that changed, and fast too.

One day, on our way back from '*lesson*' which was how we referred to extra-mural classes, a friend from school who lived in same neighbourhood started a conversation as we all strolled down the long untarred road that separated the Federal Estate from the developing Iwogban Quarters.

"Una hear about Oare Ighalo?" Evelyn, the ever informed member of the party, asked us.

"Yes o. I hear say she dey with her Aunty for Lagos" Omos added.

Evelyn looked at us with pity and laughed at our naiveté. "No be only Lag" she said sarcastically. "She don go Italy go do *ashewo*," she said casually.

"Evelyn!" I said in a loud whisper. "Stop this gist from spreading o. You know how the Ighalo boys are. I don't want any wahala o," I whispered. "The other time Judith said something about their mum and fish, Victor beat her with a whip and left her with a blood spot in her eyes" I added in trepidation.

I was really scared of the Ighalo boys. Even in their malnourished state, they were strong, terrorising the neighbourhood frequently. I knew they did not like me and my siblings. We were light-skinned and always spoke good English. So, they thought we were *forming*. Forming was street lingo for putting on airs.

I stayed out of their way even when they tried to goad me into responding. My silence infuriated them even more. I hated it when Nene sent me on errands that warranted me going to their neck of the neighbourhood and the alternative street I could take had the Aisien's huge dog that would chase anyone it saw. We heard the dog had rabies and I thought every dog on the street had rabies. I had read a novel a few years before where one of the characters had been bitten by a rabid dog. That instilled the fear of dogs in me. "You can fear" Evelyn laughed. She always spoke in Pidgin and opined that I ruined the gist with good English. "Pidgin dey make gist flow" she explained whenever I cautioned her.

"Anyway, you know say my sister dey follow one of their cousins for Western Boys High School. Na him give us the gist" she continued in a lower tone. "E talk say Oare get one Aunty wey dey stay abroad, and she come carry her go Italy to go start prostitution work."

For whatever reason, in pidgin English if you were dating someone it was referred to as following.

I looked at Evelyn in awe. It didn't make sense. The thought of anyone willingly travelling abroad to prostitute was just beyond my fourteen-year-old mind.

Apparently, Evelyn found my ignorance funny and she looked at Olohi who had been quiet all through this discussion. Olohi's mother had left the family and moved to Spain. We heard she abandoned them and travelled with a man who was a known trafficker some years ago while they were still living somewhere in Afuze. I could not confirm this, as there was no nice way to ask one of your best friends if her mother left with her pimp! Olohi told me her mum travelled to Spain to work as a hairdresser and as far as I was concerned, that was the truth.

"Evelyn, you won't mind your own business. Be spreading tales" Olohi reproached. "That was how you said Mr. Uzor, our maths teacher, was following that Nkem in SS2 because he was always giving her a ride home until we found out he was Nkem's uncle."

I laughed at this reference. It was actually a good way to shut Evelyn up because the matter got her into serious trouble.

In an all-girls school such as Idia College, we looked forward to hosting club, inter-house sports, and other inter-school functions. Those were the few opportunities we had to mingle with boys from other schools.

Nkem was the Literary and Debating Society Club president of our school, and she was very popular. The boys from Edo College and Immaculate Conception College had turned her into a legend because of her looks. She was arguably the most sought-after girl in our school. However, no one could link her with any of the boys. Then came the new mathematics teacher sent to our school by the National Youth Service Corps. In secondary schools, some female students had a knack for flirting with the teachers, especially the young corps members as well as student teachers, some of whom were stupid and exploitative. They capitalise on the innocent girls' naiveté to take advantage of them in exchange for grades, an act the school frowned upon greatly.

The new mathematics teacher was a good-looking corps member who studied engineering but was deployed to serve in our school. The girls were grateful for the corps members or corpers, as we used to call them, not because they provided cover sometimes for government's inability to provide enough teachers for schools but because they made good lunch time gossip. Lately Corper Uzor was the topic.

We noticed the very week Corper Uzor resumed work that Nkem always rode home with him in his Blue Passat TS, and my very dear Evelyn started the rumour that they were dating. This was untrue as we later found out after Nkem had gone crying to Mrs. Ero, the Vice principal, to lodge a complaint with regard to the wicked rumour.

Nkem had explained to Mrs. Ero that Uzor was her mum's younger brother who was serving the country under the NYSC scheme in Benin. It made sense that he would stay with them. He brought her to school and took her home daily.

Evelyn was expelled. It took the intervention of her father who was the school's PTA treasurer to get her back in school. You would think that would curb her gossiping excesses. Which was why she shut her mouth for a while when Olohi brought it up. She had been called out on her gossiping ways.

Evelyn was never one to give up. "I am very sure this time" she said in proper English. "I swear! You can ask any other person."

Of course, we didn't. We didn't have to. That evening, I overhead my mum discussing with another Ishan woman in my street.

"Obhio," she started, "Mrs Ighalo seems to have stopped selling fish at Oregbeni Market" Obhio meant family, and though this neighbour was in no way related to us, because she was Ishan like us so mum referred to her as Obhio.

It seemed 'obhio' had been waiting for her cue. She gave more details than Evelyn had. Mum looked at me with a stern look on her face. That was my cue to go to my room and leave the adults to continue with their discussion. Of course, I stood up and went to hide nearby to eavesdrop. I was sure Mum knew I was around listening but did not care to chastise me.

"Ighalo's daughter Oare is now in Italy o,"she said with a dramatic sigh. "I hear she is doing ashewo work there and sending dollars to her parents everyday" She sat up to make the import of the news sink in.

"Ha!" Mum exclaimed. "No wonder, I saw them making blocks and working on the house. I thought someone had bought it and was renovating…"

The neighbour quickly interrupted Mum. "They are also building a house in their village" she informed mum. "I saw Mrs Ighalo pricing Hollandaise in one store! If na before who dash monkey banana? person wey no see common London wax."

I had no idea what class of fabric London wax and Hollandaise were but from the discussion, Hollandaise was obviously more expensive than London wax.

"Na wa o! This life is something else "Mum said.

Two years later, the Ighalos moved to our street. They bought the two houses at the end of the street, knocked down a few walls, remodelled the houses and moved in. Just like that, their house became the biggest in the entire neighbourhood, and the horribly malnourished children were now chubby and looked overfed with swollen cheeks. Their stomachs were still protruded, no longer due to malnutrition but from gluttony. They wore designer items and always had a reason to throw a party. Well, with so many children, it was expected that every other month would be someone's birthday. They were more annoying now that they were rich than when they were poor.

We could hear noises their parties from way across the end of the street, loud and raucous as was to be expected. The brothers would tell anyone who cared to listen how they were moving out of the neighbourhood to one of the annexes linking GRA to Oko. Oko was one of the upcoming posh neighbourhoods that the *novueau riche* of Benin were buying properties. They talked about how the new house would have a pool, and how they would only allow certain people to visit them in their new mansion. I was sure we were not on their list, as they never invited us to any of their parties. Not that Mum would have allowed us anyway.

Mrs Ighalo was also heard telling people that she was travelling to visit her daughter abroad. We were not sure if she was aware of what her daughter did for a living or she knew and just did not care. "My pikin, Oare, go carry me sef go see all the oyinbo people," she had said proudly. "Make me by myself thank the oyinbo people wey help her start work for there."

Oare never let her visit. She consistently sent money home for the Oko property, which her greedy brothers capitalised on to milk her dry. The one they called Sunday was the ringleader. While Oare was sending in money from Italy for the Oko project, Sunday was deploying the resources to building her the house she requested and at same time a mini hostel he was building for himself somewhere at Ekenwan Road, close to the University of Benin Campus 2.

We heard Oare found out and cut him off completely. The hostel, which was already roofed, had suffered great neglect since his source of money dried up.

In a strange way I felt excited for the Ighalos because we have seen them stare poverty in the face and emerged winners. At what cost is not for us to know but to be speculated about in hushed tones.

I saw Oare when she came home for Christmas five years after her relocation. The Ighalos had moved to the new house in Oko but she came to visit old friends in the neighbourhood and, perhaps, show off a bit. She was now extremely light-skinned, wore really skimpy clothes and faux fur. She also had a fake American accent though she lived in Italy. She called everyone darling and was quite friendly whenever she visited. She stuck to the story of being a hairdresser in Italy.

Mr Ighalo still showed up in a Nissan car to Mama Efe's Bar more often than ever, now that he was retired, and his daughter had money. But, in a strange way, everything else was the same. He still got drunk most times and had one of his sons come drive him home whenever he took more alcohol than his system could cope with.

Nene still had not bought smoked fish in a long time.

Mazino Hall

People tend to complicate their own lives, as if living weren't already complicated enough.

— *Carlos Ruiz Zafón,*

Mazino Hall was on the other side of Ukpenu road. In Ekpoma, when the street extended across the highway, the other part was always called an extension. So, the students had tagged Ukpenu, then across the highway was Ukpenu extension.

Mazino Hall was one of the few luxury hostels in Ekpoma. Few students could afford it and those who could made sure everyone knew they were 'Mazinites'.

The owner of the hostel was an alumnus of the then Edo State University, currently named Ambrose Ali University after one of the former governors of the old Bendel state. His name was Ohimai Akowe. It was common knowledge that he had named the hostel after a friend of his, Zino, who was killed in crossfire between two rival cults when they were still students at the University. Zino had died in Ukpenu extension, and when Ohimai came into money, he built the hostel in memory of his friend.

Ohimai was a gentleman to the core. His being well-mannered and soft spoken could set one wondering if the terrible stories people spoke of him were true.

That he had made his money from online fraud or *yahoo-yahoo* as it was popularly called was common knowledge. The guys in the hostel spoke all the time about how he had conned some foreigners of half a billion dollar in a major scam, scammed his partners in crime and fled to some foreign country with the loot. He was there for about five years.

His family and everyone who knew him thought he was dead. Some said he had spent some years in a foreign jail. But only Ohimai knew the true story and he wasn't sharing it, at least not with us his tenants.

He was an awesome landlord though. He always had an awesome Christmas and New Year party for the students in his hostel. Students were usually allowed to have a guest. Lots of people naturally would bring a date and others had friends who did them the favours of getting an invite. The parties were awesome as they served as the means for people to unwind at the end of the year.

Ohimai was a very busy person; he had several businesses that kept him travelling frequently. So, he was rarely seen at the hostel. No one was sure where he called home as he was unmarried and had no children anyone knew of. Nevertheless, he had at some point married a German wife and some said they had a daughter.

Ohimai had someone managing the Hostel. Everyone called her Sisi Bukky.

Sisi Bukky was a class act. She was in her late thirties or early forties. She was single and always acted like she was one of the girls in the hostel. Being around students made her feel way younger, and the students indulged her.
Sisi Bukky was well travelled, or so she claimed. She would wake up with a British accent, go to bed in an American accent and several other *mélange* during the day. It was hilarious. The only constant accent was the underlying *egun* tribal accent she tried to hide in futility.

She had pictures of herself in various countries, with prominent landmarks behind her. She had a picture of hers in front of the

Eiffel Tower in France, in front of the Burj Khalifa in Dubai, on a Gondola in Venice and at Caesar's Palace in Vegas. She spoke about the day she met Celine Dion and according to her, they had spoken for a while. She always had a Celine Dion album playing in her office to confirm her attachment to the artiste.

No tale was too long or ridiculous for Sisi Bukky to tell. Truth, according to the "Mazinites," was that she was once a "madam" trafficking girls to Italy. She became friendly with Ohimai when he was in Europe. She got deported and needed a job. Ohimai gave her the role of the hostel manager. These were all Mazino Hall rumours.

The Mazino hall lobby was right in front of her office, and she could be seen exchanging money, cards and other little packages with some rich, older men, and after this exchange, some very daring Mazinite girls drove off in their exotic cars.
At first, I assumed some of the girls had their fathers or uncles visiting, and then I noticed that they always looked a little too *colourful* to be going out with their fathers in certain outfits.

Some of the girls I was friendly with who were in this racket had one sob story or the other about how things were tough back home and how they had to cater for themselves, and even sometimes their siblings. My question was always, 'Why not stay in the school hostel or one of the cheaper apartments in Ujemen?'

Ujemen which was popularly called the 'student village' was a walking distance from school as some of the indigenes rented out cheap rooms to students. Both Joyce, my classmate, who braided for other students and Victor, my dad's driver's son, who was a student and photographer lived on Poultry road in Ujemen. The

22

cost of their living there was affordable by them. They could fend for themselves. They were comparatively comfortable.

Then there was TeeKay.

Teekay or TK got her name from her initials, Tamara Kennedy. She was from the South-South and her father was a one-time minister who was filthy rich in oil money. Money was not an issue, she loved the adventure and was also a rebel.

Teekay's folks had sent her to Ekpoma after she had caused an upheaval in her boarding school in England. They decided she was better off being in a Nigerian University after that. It didn't make much difference. She had the money and lots of followers. She started an exclusive club called *crimson divas* and the girls in this strange club acted like sorority sisters and Mazino Hall was the sorority house.

The *crimson divas*, like they called themselves, had their mid finger nail painted crimson, differently from the colour of the other nails. It was their 'thing'. Guys in school were scared to date them because they were considered too formidable.

Teekay had teamed up with Sisi Bukky and they had lots of girls who could part with half their earnings if enlisted for some exclusive parties organised by politicians and other financial heavy weights. TeeKay had the contacts by virtue of her pedigree, but Sisi Bukky was the organizer based on her history as a madam.
Ohimai must have been aware of this development but chose to turn a blind eye as long as the property was maintained and there was no scandal.

My father had paid for Mazino Hall as a way of compensating me for not going to England for my studies. Owing to economic recession, we had to cut down on certain expenses. Studying in Nigeria was considered the best option. TeeKay and I were among the few whose parents were responsible for their Mazino hall bills.

I walked in on Sisi Bukky and Teekay in the middle of a chat. The latter sat on the lounge, drawing up a list. I could tell the names were those of their shortlisted candidates for a party in Abuja.

"Hello Cinderella" greeted Teekay. "Would you like to go to the ball?" She asked playfully. Sometimes I joined in the private joke. "Only if prince charming can run fast enough to stop me at midnight," I would add.

I had always wondered how fast Cinderella could possibly have run that a determined prince could not catch up with her.

Teekay did this all the time when they planned their trips. Initially I was uncomfortable with her talk about prostitution as though it were nothing. I had got accustomed to it somehow the same way I did the faint smell of marijuana that filtered through the air-conditioning vents when the girls and guys smoked behind the building.

"Not today TeeKay, not today." I said walking away.
I could hear Sisi Bukky mutter 'what a waste' and they both laughed.

The first time Teekay tried to talk me into attending one of their parties; she started with a personal question that kicked things off rather poorly.

"How much is your monthly allowance?" she asked.

That came as a shock to me. We had barely said more than a simple *hello* since I moved in and here she was asking about my finances. "I don't know why you are asking and I really don't see how it is any business of yours," I fired back.

"Easy!" she said, "it's not that big a deal. I am just curious as to how you can afford to live here and still dress in these funny Cinderella clothes," she sniggered as she looked derisively at the lovely gown my mum had got last Christmas. That look made me rethink my wardrobe for the first time.

Maybe I should be edgier with my dressing, my cousin, Amara, had once said same. Both couldn't be wrong, I reasoned. But still, who was this overdressed girl to talk to me this way.

"I love my clothes," I lied, "and for someone who thinks she has such great fashion sense, maybe you should try not to wear all your gold necklaces at once." I retorted like a child, "Your neck must hurt from the weight."

"Cinderella has got claws!" she laughed a little too loudly. "I like that," she added at the same time, giving me a sweeping look as if I was wondering how I would look after a makeover.

"What if I invite you to a birthday party in Benin?" she said unexpectedly. 'Some of the girls and I are driving to Benin. I would have to give you something appropriate to wear of course,' she added as though I had agreed already.

I really hated her guts and how she could just take over with her dark skinned good looks and caustic personality. It was rather overwhelming.

"I am not attending any party with you girls,"I knew I sounded like a child. I also knew I was fighting the urge not to run up the lobby stairs. TeeKay laughed and walked away. It continued for a while, and months later it became our private joke.

I left her and Sisi Bukky to continue whatever they were doing and headed out to the salon. Sisi Bukky and TeeKay were as thick as thieves when it came to their business. In the hostel, they had some girls who, some of us were sure, were not real students.

Some had come in as pre-degree students. Having spent their time partying and travelling throughout the semester, they could not pass their exams and had to quit school. Instead of going home, they had to continue paying their rent at Mazino Hall while parading themselves as students.

I had asked Sisi Bukky, on one of those rare occasions when we actually sat down at the lobby together, why these girls didn't just go to manage their business elsewhere. She had explained that it was good for them to be tagged students for the sake of business.

This made them marketable as these 'big men' did not want just beauty but the people they could interact with on a certain level. I had laughed at her explanation.

She sometimes had those little talks with me and treated me like I was special. I knew it was because my dad always had an envelope for her so that she could look out for me.

The Christmas party always held on the first week of December. Sisi Bukky had scheduled it such that everyone could attend as most students travelled from the second weekend in December. There was, as usual, lots of foods and drinks for the fifty students residing in Mazino Hall. But this year was a little different. According to Sisi Bukky, Ohimai had some friends who were big time investors thinking of building a hotel somewhere along Ali Street in Emaudo. They were in town and had been invited to the party.

"You all need to be at your best behaviour," she said. 'These are big men and Ohimai wants to impress them'. As she said this, she flung a knowing look at TeeKay.

"TeeKay and Obinna, both of you will assist me in making some arrangements. You know how busy I can be." she added.

Everyone knew why she needed TeeKay and Obinna.

TeeKay was to get the girls ready to strike and make some Christmas money while Obinna was to help with the entertainment and also ensure that there would be no clash between the rival cults as this clash sometimes occurred. Of course, Ohimai's guests usually had police escorts and guards, but it was wiser to prevent trouble than to manage it thereafter.

At about 3pm that fateful day, the Mazino girls scurried about with makeup as though they were models about to hit the runway. It was utter madness. Some borrowed weaves; others exchanged makeup and jewellery to complement their intended outfits. Some were on the look-out for the moneybags.

The Mazino guys were less bothered; most were on their phones trying to figure out who they could bring as dates. Some with girlfriends refused to invite their girlfriends for fear of losing them to the moneybags. I knew this from a conversation I had with Efeturi, one of the guys.

"When is Ada coming over?" I had asked, assuming his girlfriend, Ada, was his date. Both Efeturi and Ada were very close; they spent their free time together.

He had even confided in me that he would love to marry her after graduation.

"Me, bring Ada come this Christmas party?" he asked as if I was insane to contemplate such.

"Babe, you think say I dey craze? Of course I won't bring her here to be leered at by Ohimai's money-miss-road friends." He declared.

"I already told her I don't like the kind of people Ohimai brings and she suggested that Jude should come with me instead."

I mentally gave Ada thumbs up for suggesting Jude. Jude was Efeturi's friend as well as Ada's cousin. She felt Jude would protect her interests in her absence at the party, Smart girl! I wondered if Efeturi knew why she chose Jude or whether he cared.

The party was like a carnival. It was my second Mazino party but I was a bit carried away by the festivity. Mazino Hall was designed to have what one might call a courtyard. There were cobblestoned pathways leading to each of the four blocks that made up the hostel. The guys played football there sometimes. But most times people just sat out there and talked or entertained visitors.

But now it was lit with Chinese lamps and the grill was set up at one end and the cooling caravan on another.

Few garden chairs were scattered everywhere, as no one was really seated for long anyway. It was lively, it was fun, and it was a Mazino Hall party!

There were professional *suya* guys grilling the local barbecue in an assortment of beef, chicken, entrails and some parts I could not identify. You could hear the sizzle as the oil dripped from the delicious, mouth-watering meat onto the grill.

The smell of grilled meat, cigarettes and all kinds of drinks filled the air. It was 8pm and the party was just getting started. Girls scurried about in near naked state. Other girls, apart from those in '*Crimson divas,*' invited most of their friends. The male *Mazinites* also invited their male friends instead of dates. They jokingly talked about the drunken girls abandoned by the moneybags. The moneybags had arrived in a convoy of exotic cars. The girls were semi clad. This was not shocking. The guys, of course, loved the view, while some of us reclined to the shadows.

The smell of perfumes mixed with the food made the air a little too dense. I became tipsy, probably because of a glass of wine I had drunk. I hated alcohol, but at events like this I didn't want to be treated like a kid. So, I toyed with a glass of white wine.

I danced with Efeturi when the DJ played Mavin Crew's *Dorubucci*. But when Olamide's *Shakiti bobo* came on, I danced with both Efeturi and Jude simultaneously. They were both good friends of mine; so, we barely danced but goofed around with the funny dance steps.

I introduced Jude to Zainab whom I invited. Zainab loved parties from a distance. She enjoyed the buzz and the noise around it all but was actually too shy to attend any. My plan was to go back to my room to sleep if we did not like how things turned out.
The four of us were having lots of fun. None was dating anyone; we were just excited and happy that school was over.

'I won't tell Ada how much fun we had. She will be mad at me for talking her out of it,' he joked. 'Really, if I had known it would turn out this way with you guys, I would have asked her here.' I knew what he meant; we had shut out the moneybags and the skimpily clad members of *Crimson divas* and the rest of the crowd were having our own private party.

Then came the gunshots. At first, I thought it came from the people who were obviously drunk and excited. Then we heard it again. This time all doubts left those of us who were not inebriated. It was gunshot, and we scurried upstairs. We all fled and locked ourselves up in Efeturi's room. We could hear girls scream and saw people run, but we had no clue about what was going on. We were all calling parents, friends and none of us called the police.

Then just like it started suddenly, the gunshot stopped. It must have been less than five minutes, but I could have sworn it was an hour. "We should look out the window to see if there is anyone out there." Jude suggested in an almost inaudibly low tone.

"Guy, them no dey argue with gun o." Jude said, trying to trivialize the situation. Zainab was sobbing quietly; I was too shocked to do anything. Everything had happened too fast, I wasn't even sure how I climbed up the stairs. I just knew I did.

Another ten minutes of torturous wait, then we heard Sisi Bukky's voice.

She did not speak in a foreign accent, real or false. She was wailing in her local dialect and saying things we could not understand. But we somehow managed to look out of the window and saw other students. We came down the stairs and saw Ohimai in a pool of his own blood. Someone had shot him.

We were not sure who, how or when. There were, however, rumours that his former business associates assassinated him. But as usual, these were all Mazino hall rumours.

All I could think of at that point was how lucky we were to be alive. In my head I could almost hear my dad's voice amidst Sisi Bukky's wailing and all he said was 'Ofure, this is your last day at Mazino Hall'.

Then it hit me. Ohimai had died just like his friend, Zino, at Ukpenu extension, and I wondered if that meant anything.

Still Breathing

The tests of life are not meant to break you, but to make you

-Norman Vincent Peale

I was so sure I could speak Pidgin English fluently, but all that changed when I visited Warri for the first time. My folks had moved from Bariga to Muyibi Street in Ajegunle when I was three years old. For some reasons, they felt trading one slum for the other would make a difference to our financial situation, they were dead wrong!

We lived a communal life back then. Sharing facilities with neighbours and taking turn to use these facilities made you know more about your neighbours than you cared to.

I was only 13 years old when papa decided he wanted to marry another wife. His excuse was that I was still an only child after almost 15 years of marriage, worse still, a girl child. If I were, perhaps, a boy, he would think differently. Mama was very indifferent when he told her his plans, She didn't seem to care. Theirs had been an arranged marriage. She had been given to papa who was about fifteen years older to cement some family friendship and keep the miserable rubber plantation both family owned somewhere in Igieduma, a village along the Benin-Auchi highway.

Papa had always been mean to mama and never treated her with any respect. He was also a philanderer. The little he made he squandered on drinks and women. We heard his 'new wife' was a product of his wandering ways.

Her name was Ini. There were lots of stories about her. She was rumoured to be very generous with her 'favours'. She had two boys for two different fathers and the third, which she claimed was papa's heir, was on its way. Everyone assumed she was using *juju* on papa to make him marry her, but we did not think so. Funny indeed how papa loved the word, 'heir, and threw it around like there was actually an inheritance.

I think mama secretly felt sorry for Ini, knowing that once she became papa's wife, the little allowances she got from him would stop. And she would no longer be single or free to collect money from *other sources*.

I wondered how we would all live in the single room and parlour that was barely enough for the three of us. Now pregnant, Ini would be at home and mama and I would have to convert the parlour into our room. Mama decided to have a talk with papa and that move changed our life.

March is usually the hottest time of the year. The peak of the dry season and all trace of harmattan completely gone with the month of February. There was always that stillness of air. The heat was sweltering, and you could actually tell the breeze had stopped blowing completely because the trees were still, not a leaf or a branch moved.

Mama had made yam porridge and as was her common practice, she had seasoned it with the popular scent leaf. It was one of papa's favourite meals. It was obvious she wanted to butter him up for the discussion. Papa had come back from bank, where he worked as a driver. This was a little earlier than usual because his boss had travelled out of the country.

"Have you fetched water for your father?"
Mama had asked me to take the blue plastic bucket with the metal handle filled with water to the bathroom at the back of the building. I was also to make sure nobody used it. I told her I had

done as instructed and stayed outside. She nodded. I went outside to talk with Kemi, my neighbour's daughter. Kemi and I were very close and always talked about 'making it' and moving up to Ladipo which was a lot less rowdy and actually a better neighbourhood. For us, Ikoyi was too far a dream, Apapa was as close as we dared.

I left Kemi to eavesdrop on papa and mama's conversation and, after a while, I could hear them clearly.

"So, you want to carry Onayimi to Warri?" He asked calmly.

"I just think this house will be too small for us." Mama explained. She had already told me, and I was quite excited about it, and was really hoping papa would not stop it from happening.

"Your new wife will soon have a baby, and she will need someone to help her," mama continued "so I am going to Igarra, while Onayimi can stay in Warri with Ozavize and her family."

Papa thought for a while, and I am sure the selfish wheel in his head was spinning really fast. Despite his having fewer burdens, he could focus on Ini whom we heard was leaving her two boys with her mother in Eket.

"That is fine." Papa said without any hesitation, "as long as you don't go about telling people in Igarra that I drove you out when I married a new wife o! Because that would be a lie," he said with some seriousness.

"I can take care of my family as a man." He said with pride.
"Of course not, I will tell them Onayimi is going to live with Ozavize so she can know her cousins better. I just want to go and rest in the village a bit so that you and the *iyawo* can have some

35

time to know yourselves." She said like the dutiful wife of days gone by.

It is amazing what mothers could and would dutifully tolerate from their husbands. Those were simpler times when men thought themselves gods and women subservient.

The day mama and I left Muyibi was the last day I stepped into that house. I never looked back. I knew I would keep in touch with Kemi. I knew I would make something of myself, I also knew that Muyibi was only a colourful part of my story. Mama moved to the village, and I moved to Warri.

I met Fanen the first day at school in Warri. He was the *Hausa* boy in our class. Actually, Fanen was from Benue State, but as far as everyone from the South was concerned, he might as well be from Sokoto or Borno. No one cared to know.

It reminded me of all the times in Lagos that people of the *Yoruba* tribe would refer to my family as *omo ibo* . There are three major tribes in the country and several minorities , but to the average *Yoruba* man, there were only three tribes; the *Yoruba* and every other person who could either be *Hausa* or *Ibo*. So, I could see how in Warri they felt Fanen was *Hausa*.

Fanen was my academic rival from the first day we had a test in class. He had been the smartest kid in the class before I arrived. I was the new girl and I was already his competitor. He didn't like that one bit. So, he challenged me at every opportunity. I heard of Czechoslovakia for the first time from him. He would come with a new word each day, just to ask if I knew what it meant or if I could spell it.

'Do you know the meaning of despondent,' he asked on a Monday morning.

On the Tuesday of that week, he also asked, 'have you ever heard of the word Eleemosynary?' I wasn't really sure if he knew these words or he just dug them up each day to bother me.

This particular day was a Friday and as usual he wanted to know if I could spell Czechoslovakia. Of course, I couldn't and till date I still get the spelling mixed up as an adult.

However, that was all Fanen needed to gloat. He needed to take back his position as the smartest student in class. I was getting bored by his pettiness with the rivalry. So, it was a win-win for both of us as his friends hailed him.

His joy was short lived because that was the day I learnt my mother had died in her farm in Igarra. That was the day I understood what it meant to feel so much pain until it numbed your senses.

Aunty Ozavize and her husband were very supportive and loving, but they were not rich. They had their own responsibilities. Mama used to send my fees and little pocket money realized from the proceeds of her trade in the village. Aunty Ozavize came to take me home from school that day and I wondered if I was ever going back there. I dreaded the thought of going back to Lagos to live with papa and Ini, barely a year after leaving them.

Maybe Mama wasn't dead after all; maybe those Bible stories we read of people coming back to life would happen. God knew mama had to take care of me, so he would not take her just like that.

It is hard to grieve when you still nursed the slightest hope of a resurrection, but even hope eventually gets struck down by death in times like these.

Mama's funeral was small and private. Most of the villagers showed up; yet, it was a moderate affair. Papa came and sat down silently, not sure of what to do with this news. But he tried to look as broken as a widower was expected to. I looked at him and knew it was an act. I knew because he never bothered to send us any money, he never cared to find out how we were doing. He was obviously happy we left Lagos for him and his new wife.

I hated him as though he killed mama. If he had loved her or treated us better, mama wouldn't have been in the farm on the day she died. She would not have been bitten by a snake. She would have been alive, and I would not have had to stand over her coffin or drop a handful of earth on it while the priest said, *dust to dust.*

Papa and I had not spoken at all since he came to Igarra the night before, and I had nothing to say to him even as we walked back to the house in the village. I stared at the rocks and remembered the stories mama told me as a child. She told me how almost all the houses in Igarra had two floors because lions would come from the mountains and terrorise the villagers. If Mama could read, I would say she probably read John Henry Patterson's *Man Eaters of Tsavo* or seen the screen adaptation of *The Ghost and the Darkness* in which Val Kilmer was starred.

Maybe it did happen like she said.

"Onayimi , you will have to come back to Lagos." Papa said finding his way into my thoughts. "Abi you want to stay in Warri?" He asked, almost immediately.

I knew he wanted me to know I had that option, but my fear was if I stayed in Warri, would he pay my fees? Not that I was sure of whether or not going back to Lagos meant he would either. I was just about to write my Junior Secondary School exams and I had no idea if that would be the end of my education. I was only fourteen and I felt like I was Atlas with the world on his shoulder.

I remembered those days, in Muyibi Street, when I was carefree. I remembered Kemi and how we planned to buy houses in Ladipo or some other streets in Apapa by the time we were older and richer. I had kept in touch with Kemi for some time back then. It was not convenient writing letters and having spare cash for the postage stamp. So, the letters became less frequent, unless I saw someone who lived in the old neighbourhood who could deliver a letter to her.

She had written a letter through papa, trying to console me on mama's passing. I read it twice and made a mental note to add it to her previous letters.

"I will think about it, papa. Let me finish my Junior WAEC and talk to Aunty Ozavize." I said calmly.

Papa shrugged and went into the house. He left for Lagos two days later and I never saw him till his funeral five years later. He sent me money once when Aunty Ozavize went to Lagos and caused a scene and that was that.

I went back to school and some of the students in my class came to console me at my desk. Some just looked at me with pity. Even Fanen had stopped the rivalry and bought me lunch twice that week. Just before our exams, I mentioned to Ejiro, my closest friend in class that I might not be able to continue with school.

"Why you go dey talk like that na?" she asked in her warri accent. "As you know book reach, you go just let am waste?" she scolded me for wanting to give up as smart as I was.

"Ejiro, no be my fault," I said, trying to hold back the tears, 'na who go pay my school fees?" I asked. "My pa say make I come back to Lagos, and I know say e no go pay."

Ejiro looked at me sadly and furrowed her brow for a few seconds like one deep in thoughts.

"Maybe you fit work gather small money." She suggested.

"Where will I find work?" I asked. It seemed oddly exciting that there might be that possibility.

"You fit do sales girl na, I pass Fanen Mama shop the other day. Them write say them need sales girl." Before I could say anything, we saw Fanen and a group of his friends and Ejiro shouted his name "Fanen! guy show abeg we wan ask you something."

He walked towards us, "Onayimi, how are you doing? Have you managed to copy the notes I gave you?" He asked, referring to the notes he lent me on subjects I missed while I was away for Mama's funeral.

I was about to respond when Ejiro cut in, "Abeg no be note make I call you. Una fit continue una *efiko* gist after." Ejiro thought Fanen and I were the definition of *efiko*, bookworms.

"Fanen, your ma put sales girl sign for her shop, you fit help Onayimi get the job?" She asked bluntly.

She spoke on my behalf, as I was too embarrassed to say I would need to work to pay my fees.

"I don't know if she has found someone yet," he started. But Ejiro cut him short again, "I pass there this morning the sign still dey there make you ask your ma." She snapped "Abi you want make Onayimi no go school?" She asked obstinately.

"Ejiro, cool down." Fanen said, you could tell he was getting upset "I go ask when I reach house." he answered back in pidgin. I managed to say '*thank you*' and he nodded and left us alone.

Ejiro laughed as he glared at her, "No mind am jare. Na so e go dey do *aje butter.*"

Aje butter was a street term used to describe privileged kids.

"You harsh o!" I spoke, now that she let me speak. 'It's not his fault that I cannot pay my fees, why you come dey shout for am like that'.

"It's not your fault either." She said with some empathy. "But we have to find a solution."

I hugged her. It was so sweet to have someone other than Aunty Ozavize look out for me. It meant a lot.

"Oya, e don do." She switched back to pidgin. "Fanen no buy you lunch today?" She added mischievously.

We both laughed as she playfully tried to call him back. Ejiro's theory was that Fanen "liked" me, and mama's death was just the right opportunity for him to show affection without drawing any attention. 'You be fine girl, Fanen na fine boy and two of una like book. Una love go too make sense!' she said with excitement.

Most of the girls in JSS3 had boyfriends, some more than one. At fourteen, I didn't have one and I didn't want one. I just wanted to go to school and never be poor again. I wanted more than anything to be successful and have people talk about how well I had done for myself.

Fanen talked his mum into giving me the job. Aunty Ozavize was not too thrilled that I had to work, but she also knew the options we had were limited. I certainly did not want to go and live with papa in Lagos.

We moved to Kolokolo, a neighbourhood in Warri that reminded me of Ajegunle. Aunty Ozavize's husband had lost his job when the Nigerian Telecommunications Limited, NITEL, went under. Salaries had been owed for so many months, so it didn't make any immediate financial impact when they laid him off. The entire household had been living on Aunty's meagre salary as a secondary school teacher in one of the public schools close to Jakpa road.

"I know you will do well, Onayimi." Aunty Ozavize said somberly. "I just wish you didn't have to do this as it will mean less time for studies and I know how much my sister wanted you to go to school. Don't worry, Aunty. I know how much mama wanted this too and I won't let her down."

I didn't earn much money, but what I earned was enough to pay my fees and buy a few books. Fanen must have told his mum about my pitiable plight because she always had something extra for me. Foodstuff and some groceries each month. This went on for two years till it was time to prepare for my Senior School Certificate Exam. Then she called me to have a chat.

"Onayimi, I have found a replacement for you now that you have to prepare for exams." She said, and my heart sank. I wasn't ready to quit. I still needed the money desperately to pay for the exams and save up for university tuition.

"Please ma, I will not allow studies to affect work. I will come after school and weekends as usual.." She smiled and hushed me to silence 'my dear, you are a very special child. The last two years have been very easy for me because of your hard work, but you cannot play with your final exams,' she handed me an envelope which I opened and found the teller for payment of my exam fees. I was speechless, but my tears said it all.

"I went to pay Fanen's fees and I paid yours too." She said, smiling at my dumbstruck reaction. "Just read well and excel." She advised me.

I started crying even harder as I hugged her. I still couldn't speak. I could close from school, go home and actually study for my exams. 'Thank you ma, I don't know how else to show my gratitude,' I said, in tears. 'Please if you need me at the store anytime, I will come and help out.'

"I won't need you at the store, Yimi!" She laughed. "Study hard and make us proud." she encouraged me.

Aunty Ozavize and I did a funny jig when I went home to tell her the good news, and she launched into prayer mode.

"Our God Almighty will help her and prosper her." she said, kneeling down with her hands raised to heaven.

"In her time of need, God will send her help. She will find favour in the sight of God and man." She continued for the next five minutes in her prayer which I punctuated with a resounding *amen.*

I read for my exams with great enthusiasm, and planned on sending a message to papa. Maybe he would be proud at the opportunity of my going to the university and offer some help.

Kemi, my old friend had introduced me to e-mails and Fanen had helped me to understand the use of computer and internet. Initially, he would help me send emails to Ejiro. But one day he told me I had to learn how to do it myself.

"Yimi, I am not your secretary." He said playfully. "You need to learn how to send emails yourself. The computer won't bite you. Besides, I know those tame messages you ask me to send are not your real thoughts." He kidded.

I was a bit nervous at first as he had to sit rather close to me. I realized I wasn't a kid anymore and maybe I did want a boyfriend. I wanted to gist with Kemi via email about my amazing 'friend', Fanen. I knew I could not ask Fanen to send emails that had him mentioned so, I decided I would learn so I can send messages privately to Kemi.

The first email I sent all on my own was from a cybercafé and it was sent to Kemi. The café had charged by the hour and I was very slow at typing. So, it seemed more like a telegram at the end of the hour purchased.

Hello Kemi,

The owner of the shop where I work has paid for my SSCE, I told you she is Fanen's mum, right?

Fanen taught me how to use the computer, so this mail I am sending is all typed by me!

I think Ejiro has been right all along, Fanen likes me and I am beginning to like him too!

Don't worry. I am still preparing for UNIBEN. I still want to be a doctor, and we will still be roommates!

I have to go now. I pray we pass and there is money for school fees.

Miss you always,

Ps: We will still buy the house in Apapa, or maybe we can move to the Island.

Yimi

The mail took me almost an entire hour to type, but I left the cybercafé very proud of my successful mailing skills. It felt like I just acquired a super power.

I didn't have a lot of emails, so I would buy an hour worth of cyber time and use it for an entire week! I would read Kemi's emails, reply to and go back home. I did this twice each week and I looked forward to the emails.

Exams came and results followed after a few months. In those few months, I went back to work in one of the new Cybercafés as an attendant. The pay was small, but I had access to internet facilities and would chat with Kemi and Fanen, though the latter and I saw sometimes.

Fanen and I passed all our exams but Ejiro had to write the exams again as she had failed English Language and another subject which she must pass to gain admission into a higher institution. Fanen was registered for the University Matriculation Examination and gained admission to study Mechanical Engineering at the University of Benin. Aunty Ozavize had advised that I wait to have my SSCE results before being registered for UME. This, she explained, was to save paying twice if I was unsuccessful. Kemi, like Fanen, passed both and also gained admission to UNIBEN to study Accounting. I felt a bit sad that I had to wait an extra year, but I felt worse knowing I wasn't even certain of how my tuition and accommodation would be paid for.

On a Sunday, just after service, I went to thank Fanen's mum for her help and tell her about my success. She was so excited that he brought out a bottle of fruit wine. She asked the maid to bring me a plate of rice and chicken stew. I declined shyly and she gave me a bag of groceries to take home to Aunty Ozavize. This was the practice whenever I visited.

I was about to leave when Fanen stopped me. He was looking buff like he had been working out, probably to impress the girls at UNIBEN. I thought about this with a twinge of jealousy. He even had a mobile phone now with the presence of the Global System for Mobile Communications in Nigeria.

"Yimi, I need to show you something." He said excitedly as he pulled me to the dinning section where he had his laptop open.

"I have been searching for local scholarships online, and I found some which I think you should apply for." He was so excited that you would think I had be awarded one of the scholarships already.

I applied for two of them. One was from a South-South group, and another from an oil servicing firm.
I got neither of them.

University matriculation exam results were out. I did very well, but as usual papa said he did not have money for my education. He suggested that I should learn a trade instead. He tried to convince aunty Ozavize to look for a good fashion school or hairdresser, where she could sign an agreement on my behalf as an apprentice.

I cried my heart out that night as there was nothing I could do. I contemplated taking to papa's advice that I should learn a trade with the little money I had saved up. Almost immediately, I decided against it and kept my job at the cybercafé to save up a bit more while taking advantage of the free internet. I searched online for scholarships daily till I found one with my state government. I applied with a very touching cover letter attached to my application and statement of my impressive secondary school leaving certificate results. I got the scholarship. Fund was enough to take care of tuition and accommodation. It was a miracle, but I had already lost another year when this happened.

I left for Benin the next day as admission was almost closed. I still had my name on the list of those who gained admission to study medicine. Papa did not attend my matriculation. Maybe he was ashamed that I was going to be a medical doctor. A dream that was fast becoming a reality and he had contributed nothing to.

I started the journey to becoming a medical doctor at nineteen; I also became an orphan at nineteen. Papa's death meant little to me as he died the day I left Lagos six years earlier. Nevertheless, I felt alone in a strange way. But I wasn't completely alone as I had Aunty Ozavize, Kemi and of course, Fanen.

The New Benin Market

Men, it has been well said, think in herds; it will be seen that they go mad in herds, while they only recover their senses slowly, one by one

— *Charles Mackay*

Everyone had walked away from the scene, but not without one self-righteous comment or the other. For some strange reason I stood transfixed. I could not walk away. It seemed so insensitive. There he was in pain; badly bruised from the beating he had been given. Maybe the police would be a welcome relief for once, but not their being around would make much. Even if they would show up, comical in their usually dirty and worn out uniforms, it would be when everything had obviously been taken care o. It's easy to blame the police, but they are a product of our society. I used to ponder on why anyone would want to be a policeman in this country, but then the job market was not exactly stacked with jobs. This had even been the case before the current economic meltdown.

The man in question had robbed a market stall and stolen a tuber of yam! This, to most people, was a stupid act. But I felt hunger could make one stupid and, in a rowdy market place, he might as well have committed murder. Even the pickpockets in the crowd would be the first set of people to cast a stone!

"My children never chop, abeg na hunger cause am." He said, hoping that someone in the maddening crowd would listen. I could hear him and even understand his plight, but you dared not interfere with the mob, or you risked getting beaten as well. I knew how it feels to be hungry without any idea of where the next meal would come from. The look of the man moved me. I had seen a similar look before. I had seen it in my dad's eyes when the soup

56

was all watery, with some vegetables floating in it. I had seen that look when we came up with one demand or the other and he was totally clueless as to how his paltry savings was going to transform into decent cash.

I definitely knew that look. It was despair, hopelessness and helplessness, all rolled into a ball of misery.

I was the last child in a family of four children, with everything at my disposal till tragedy struck. I used to wonder how less privileged people survived in the face of insufficiency. I never knew that life till lately. I learnt about hand-me -downs, and how for new clothes, they would go to the bend down select or okrika corner of the popular new Benin market. These were used clothes brought into the country and usually displayed on old cartons and on the ground in various markets. You would have to bend and make your pick from the colourful array, hence the name bend down select. You could see the excited trader draw attention to his wares with his crude charm.

"Madam make you come select for junior."

"We get oga size today o!"

Breaking into my thoughts was the police who came, angry looking and perhaps wondering why the mob did not set the man ablaze with a tyre like they used to do. Given this, the police would not have much to do as the robber's charred corpse would be the responsibility of the local government council.

"Oya stand up, useless man. Na so una go dey thief?" The police officers said grudgingly, dragging the bruised and battered man along. I walked slowly to my car in tears. What he did was wrong, I would never condone stealing under any circumstance, but I could understand how too poor one had to be to steal a tuber of yam to feed his family members. At 15, I had already experienced what having it all looked like. I had attended the best private schools; I had the most colourful birthday parties held in my honour; I had travelled quite a bit. But now, as I walked from Iyaro to New Benin to board a bus to Ramat Park, I looked at the other Idia College girls who were with me at the scene and it hit me afresh as to how how one could easily lose everything.

"You kids are just spoilt." Aunty Edna yelled at me. As far as she was concerned, wearing decent clothes, eating a good meal and having the guts to ask older ones some rather daring questions made us spoilt and over pampered. Not that I really cared what she thought because I was 10 years old, smarter than most kids in my class, had more clothes and shoes than most kids I knew and I was as happy as I could be.

What had brought about the huge hoopla was my divulging her age to my neighbour's maid, Joy.

Aunty Edna was twenty four and she spent several long weekends with us back in the day. Quite a 'village smart', so she would easily

56

bully Joy who was rather timid. Joy let her get away with it because she thought Edna was older, but with my 'big mouth', I had let the cat out of the bag, and Edna had lost her bullying rights. So naturally she was furious.

'So we be mate self!' Joy screeched in her shrill voice 'and when Aunty give us something I dey let you chose before me,' she managed in English, because her madam had forbidden her from speaking Pidgin English around the kids. Joy and Aunty Edna made the English Language sound like some alien dialect , and when they got stuck trying to speak it, they would mutter inaudibly under their breath, and as mischievous little critters that we were, we would ridicule them endlessly. Little wonder why they looked for every possible reason to make us cry while our folks were out.

Maybe we had all we needed, and, to some, it might have made us seem like over pampered kids, but it was definitely not true, because my parents were strict and hardworking people, who made sure we did our chores. There was a maid, but each person had to pull their weight around the house. We studied hard, played a little and watched television a lot!

I still recall Sesame Street, New zoo review, Muppets and all those fun and educative TV shows which we grew up to love. I was a book and TV addict as a kid. My parents did not seem to mind, as long as it kept us indoors.

Growing up in Benin City like I did was a lot of fun. I can still remember birthday parties in school. Then I used to look forward to weekends because there used to be outings lined up by my dad for my brothers and me. Saturdays were awesome as long as daddy was in town, or else it would be hell with my older brothers and Aunty Edna always on our tail.

It was shortly after my eleventh birthday; papa had come home and called my eldest brother, Oshomah, to the study. Oshomah was only 16 at the time and had just gained admission to the University of Benin to study Law. The twins, Ojior and Omoh, were both in SS1 at Greater Tomorrow while I was in JSS1 in same school. In the 90's, few private secondary schools existed and GT was top-notch in Benin.

Dad came home a bit earlier than usual and he didn't smile. He didn't come in with his usual bag of goodies. Neither did he respond to my greetings.

'Oshomah, I have to go to the hospital,' dad said in a voice that was barely audible. 'Your mum had an accident. I don't have much information yet, but stay by the phone in case I need you to do anything while I am away'. He continued in an even lower tone. 'Don't mention this to the twins or Oshioke yet.'

At the mention of my name, I quickly walked away from the door of the study where I had stood motionless for a few minutes. I hadn't meant to eavesdrop. I was going to meet papa when they started talking, and something in his tone had made me stay rooted on the spot. It had an ominous ring to it and I feared for mama's health and safety.

What happened to her? What kind of accident? She was fine when she left for the office this morning.

I said a silent prayer as I ran up to my room.

The accident in question was a stroke. Mum had mysteriously suffered a stroke that had left her paralysed on one side .She could neither walk nor talk and we had to take care of her as we would do an invalid. It was difficult to see mama in this condition as she had to be carried or supported around the house. We had to feed her and I just could not understand how this happened. Mum was the disciplinarian in the house; she was the one who put us back in line when we strayed. She it was who made sure everyone pulled their weight around the house with chores and school.

Who would push us to get ready on Sundays for church? Who would tell Aunty Joy what meal to prepare? It felt strange knowing mama could not do so many things and she was right there in the house and not on a trip. But that was only the beginning.

Two months later, daddy lost his job at the firm where he worked as the Chief Financial Officer.

The company had made some major cases of fraud that alerted the Financial Crimes Commission. Some of the documents signed had implicated dad in a major scandal. The board needed a scapegoat to appease their stakeholders and papa was the fall guy. Dad was suspended pending further investigations and things took a whole new turn for us.

We all knew whenever dad called a family meeting; it was usually some depressing news. If it were good news, he never called for a meeting; rather, he would excitedly blurt it out without a formality. "I know the last few months have been difficult." He said, his voice sounded shaky. "I am trying my best to clear my name in this scandal but it is taking a while. The Financial Crimes Commission have ordered our account frozen till when this is resolved."

"We need to take turns in taking care of your mother a lot more now as we have to make some changes around the house." He cleared his throat as we all stared at him in consternation. "Oshoke, Ojior and Omoh will have to change schools and go to a public school from next term." he paused to let this sink in. Then he looked at Oshomah. "I am selling off your mother's car so we can have some cash at hand while we resolve this mess."

Oshomah was upset but kept calm when he spoke. "Dad, that has been my means of getting myself transported school since mama had the stroke." He said.

"You will have to join the bus, or when I sell the car we can pay for some accommodation close to school." He explained with so much pain in his voice. I could not bring myself to complain that it would be humiliating changing to a public school.

That was not all. 'We also have to let Joy go,' he declared. 'There is no child in the house. We can all look after ourselves as that is an added expense that is not necessary at this time,' he explained.

This was all too much to take at once and I started crying. I wasn't really sure why but I couldn't hold back the tears anymore. Did this mean we were poor?

Would we have to move out of the house too and go to live in some strange neighbourhood or an attic like that of V.C Andrews' novel, Flowers in the Attic. Or did dad not die like the father in the book? We perhaps stood a chance. But dad did not say anything after that but he walked into his room and shut the door for the rest of the day. I looked at my brother; nobody said a word.

New term came and I resumed at Idia College which was my mum's Alma mater. I had heard so much about the Appian Way that I felt like I had been there before. Mum had told me how the trees made the Appian Way such a beautiful sight and she was right. The school hall was on the left hand side of it and the assembly ground on the right. It was just a long stretch of tarred road with trees on both sides, but it gave the school a view Monet would be proud to paint. I liked the Appian Way but did not like the fact that I was in a public school.

Things did not get better as quickly as papa assumed.

Ojior and Omoh started attending Edokpolor Boys Secondary School and they could barely enrol for their senior secondary school exams when it was time to do so. Oshomah had a hard time coping in the University with no money. Mama was not getting any better and papa was not getting any closer to being vindicated. I woke up each day to help clean mama up and do some other chores before getting ready for school. Dad would feed her and take care of her while we were gone for the day. Sometimes kind sisters from church or some female relatives would come and help us out. You could see the pity in their eyes as they wondered how it got to this. We wondered same.

One of the sisters from our church suggested a deliverance session and papa initially scoffed at the suggestion. Sister Maduagu was not one to give up easily. Months later, she came to help out at home and she called dad to the back of the house for private conversation but she had picked the wrong spot as they were behind my bedroom window. I heard everything they said.

'Brother Etokhana,' she addressed him as brother with reference to the church. 'We have been watching these happenings in your home go on for close to a year. First, it was your wife, then your job and things have continued going down,' she stated the obvious. 'We had this conversation a few months ago and you said they were mere coincidences and that it would be fine soon. So I left you alone,' she paused, trying to read papa's reaction to know if it was necessary to continue.

Dad was broken at this point; so, he listened. Failing this, he would have scoffed at how people read ominous meanings to things that can easily be explained, but he wasn't scoffing; life had taught him not to scoff.

'We had a prayer meeting last Friday and it was revealed after a fast that your family is under attack by the enemies, but God is delivering your family of these attacks in Jesus name,' she said in a loud voice that made me certain the enemies would be at least startled.

I said a quiet 'Amen' and to my surprise I heard papa say so too. Things must be even worse than I thought. Dad went to church on Sundays. He was a Christian but he didn't do much else for the faith. Mum was the one who pushed us to participate in more church activities; she was in some prayer groups and would fast on different occasions and encourage us to try too.

It was rather ironic that she was the one worst hit by the said attack. 'We want to ask you and your children, even sister Etokhana to fast for seven days in the coming week,' she said in a tone that made me a bit uneasy. 'All of you must stay at home and fast, pray and cry to God to visit your family. Our prayer group will be joining you and on the seventh day we will come to this house and pray for the final deliverance.'

Dad must have nodded his agreement because I did not hear his response. I wondered what my brothers would say about it.

Ojior and Omoh were at home, not doing much as they were waiting for their results. I was on holiday already, so all we would need to do would be to pull Oshomah from school for an entire week.

Dad went to mama's room after Sister Maduagu had left. I could hear him talk to her. We all did that sometimes. She could hear and understand, but just couldn't speak clearly. He was most likely telling her about the fast.

Oshomah hated being away from school, but the last two years had been so hellish for our family that papa had to take up a teaching job in a private school. It was strange how everyone abandoned us. Not even Aunty Edna visited anymore. Very few uncles or dad's friends stopped by occasionally. Long gone were those weekends when mum and Aunty Joy would cook tirelessly as if we were throwing a party as dad's friends would come over to the house to eat, drink and discuss sports and politics while we vacated the living room for them.

Mum loved playing hostess and she enjoyed cooking and hearing them comment on her amazing cooking. We always had ingredients for Isi-ewu, fish and assorted meats for different types of pepper soups while dad kept the bar and the fridge stocked with drinks.

It always appeared there was a party unless dad was out of town. Then it would be just us. Now, it's barely two years ago; it felt like a lifetime. It takes crises to know those whose loyalty you can count on.

'The boys,' as mum fondly called my brothers, and I sat in the living room and talked like we sometimes did.

"It has reached fasting stage." Ojior said. He was a bit of a rebel and was certainly not looking forward to the fast. Omoh was more level headed, but would never go against Ojior; so he remained silent. He had told me earlier that if this was what it would take, it made sense for everyone to do it.

Oshomah walked towards mum's room and, like a shepherded flock of sheep, we followed. They stood while I sat beside mum on the bed. She managed a rueful smile. We all kept silent, not a word was said but we all knew what each one of us was thinking. We would do this not because we were eating meals that lacked any real form of nourishment. We would do this not because we had to take public transport, go to public school and live below the standard we were used to. We would do it for mum.

"We will start the fast on Monday." Oshomah said with such authority that he sounded so much like dad.

We all nodded. Not even Ojior could say anything contrary.

We started the fast on Monday and, of a truth, it saved us some foodstuff as well. Also, it brought us as family members closer. We all stayed indoors, read the bible passages given by the prayer group in church and prayed every three hours-the hours of prayer. Even mum had to join in the fast, and I could tell she approved of it.

On the third day of the fast, mum said 'Amen' when we prayed. Excited by this, we all paused in the middle of the prayer. The smile on mum's face told us we were not mistaken. If we had any doubts about the fast, it fast faded and was over taken by hope and faith in the prayers we made.

Dad made us take turns in the prayer sessions; we faithfully read the bible passages and hoped for a miracle. With each day, mum seemed stronger and could say a few words. She always called dad *Obi'm* which was the Igbo word for "my heart" before she had the stroke. Mum was Ibo, but one would think she was from Auchi with the way she spoke the language. 'Obim', her pet name for dad, was her very first clearly audible word as she regained her speech.

Dad had tears in his eyes when she called him just after the late prayers on Thursday. He walked towards her and hugged her. It was such an emotional sight. Oshomah asked us to let them be.

"Wow!" Ojior always had something to say "mum is talking! I can't believe I have actually missed her yelling at me and complaining pretty much about everything I do."

We all laughed and it dawned on me that the depression seemed to be easing off. We were still broke and could not afford a decent meal, but we were close-knit and happier.

On Saturday, dad went out and bought frozen turkey and some vegetables. He even bought a few drinks and said we would celebrate the end of the fast, and since it was a Sunday and the prayer group would be coming to break the fast after church with us, we should be ready to host them. I was busy with the boys. We sliced the vegetables for the fried rice and we grilled the chicken with lots of pepper, garlic powder and barbeque sauce and way mum liked it that way. We were in a festive mood and everyone was excited.

Sunday morning, the seventh day of the fast, I thought I would have a heart attack. I walked to the living room at 6 a.m. for the morning prayers, and just as we settled in, someone shuffled in slowly. It was mum! Dad rushed to her to assist her. 'Oluchi, you could have asked me to help you,' he said with so much joy and fear at same time. Mum could move without being assisted, but she had not moved by herself for a long time. It was shocking to see her move without being supported. We all started to scream and talk at same time until mum said, 'we must pray now.'

Never had the heavens felt such joy in the way we praised and worshiped that morning. It was just one week and I wondered if this had been done earlier, or this was the time God wanted it to happen; it was indeed God's time for us. The final prayer session was over and you could feel there was a presence beyond us in the room. The prayer was given the liberty to coordinate this session. There was a lot of 'casting out and binding'.

People were speaking in tongues and we heard mum join in. she was singing and crying; it was like she was not herself. I opened my eyes and I could see the twins were as shocked as I was. Then there was a loud scream but later there was utter silence. You could hear a pin drop. I could hear my heartbeat and I feared the others could hear it too. Then the leader of the prayer group said in a tired voice, 'it is over; we have won the battle.' We sang songs of praise and later sat down quietly to eat. It felt very odd and strangely exhausting.

The next day there was news on the radio. Dad's firm, with the assistance of the FCC, had been able to uncover the real culprits behind the fraud. It therefore asked all suspended staff members to resume with immediate effect. All allowances and salaries were paid.

I heard mum call Ojior, her speech was getting better and I was certain a few days of yelling at the boys would make her speech fine.

When Love Is Not Enough

Has he ever trapped you in a room and not let you out?
Has he ever raised a fist as if he were going to hit you?
Has he ever thrown an object that hit you or nearly did?
Has he ever held you down or grabbed you to restrain you?
Has he ever shoved, poked, or grabbed you?
Has he ever threatened to hurt you?
If the answer to any of these questions is yes, then we can stop wondering whether he'll ever be violent; he already has been.

-Lundy Bancroft

S

he sat by the window, with the blind pulled aside. Her head rested on the window pane. Staring out in the pouring rain, she looked like a painter's masterpiece, her sadness well captured in the hypothetical canvas.

Ainehi was no painter's model. Admittedly, her striking beauty, wide eyed innocence and graceful mien would make her suitable. Ironically, the sadness in her eyes did nothing to dent her striking presence. She had been sitting on the very same spot for over an hour, waiting for her husband, Kome.

She hadn't bothered to set the dinner table tonight; he had sent her a text message which read, 'Don't wait up.' 'How civil of him,' she thought cynically. It was past midnight and she was waiting. She knew she had to tell him tonight or lose her courage. She most likely would get a beating, or maybe he would plead and beg like he sometimes did. With Kome, one was never completely sure. Whatever happened, she would be free at dawn. She was certain of this. She contemplated going to bed and leaving him a note in the morning on her way out she. But she decided against it almost immediately. She needed to do this face to face, for closure. Kome had always been like this. Everyone knew that and warned her but Ainehi had always thought his love for her and marriage would change him eventually. But this was wishful thinking.

Ainehi and Kome had met 5 years ago at the university. Kome was just about to graduate as a Mechanical Engineer while Ainehi was in her third year as a Law student. They had both met when Kome offered to pay for her lunch at one of the popular eateries. In retrospect, she should have said a firm 'No' and thereby saved herself several years of abuse.

Kome had been very determined to woo her. Good looking in a debonair manner that was uncharacteristic of most of the guys in the Engineering faculty, he was always well dressed. His shirt was almost always neatly tucked in. he never thought 'dirty jeans' was the approved uniform for all engineers like some of his peers. He spoke calmly and seemed very sure of himself.

On their third date, he had told her his plans for the future-what he expected of his dream home, wife, and kids. He had painted a very surreal but realistic image. Before the date was over, Ainehi could see herself cast for a role in the movie. She wanted to be "Mrs Kome."

Signs of Kome's Jekyll and Hyde personality began to surface about 5 months into their relationship. She had hitched a ride with a course mate from the Law Faculty to the private hostel. Kome who was waiting for her in his car, parked in front of her hostel, was livid. 'So you are now fooling around with course mates,' he said coldly 'is this what you intend doing when, after I might have graduated, you are here all by yourself?' She wasn't sure he was talking to her in that tone. It was very unlikely. 'Kome, is everything okay?' she asked.

"I should be asking you that." He said, his voice raised. In his eyes, he had a look which she had never seen before. He was angry. It was almost funny because she had no idea of why he was mad at her.

She tried to make light the situation by teasing him a bit. "Is my jealous boyfriend angry that his hot girlfriend has an admirer?" She had never thought a slap could come so fast. Her face stung from the slap and Kome walked into his car and drove off without a word. She was stunned, hurt and too shocked to cry or even understand what had happened. A minute later, she was excited about coming home to Kome and wanted to make lunch for them both. The next minute she was standing in front of her room, holding her face in confusion. There had to be an explanation for this, but she wasn't going to listen to it because she was done. No man had the right to hit her. Not even a husband, much less a 5 month old boyfriend. Ainehi blamed herself for not seeing those jealous traits earlier in

Kome.

Well, he would never hit her again, she thought. Kome called incessantly the rest of the day, sent her messages on her blackberry, came over to the hostel with flowers and chocolates and, like all abusers, had a sob story. She fell for it then and several other times in the years to come.

She had dated Kome for about three years before they got married, and in those three years, Kome was the most romantic, passionate and temperamental person she had ever encountered. She talked about leaving him several times. She had him arrested once and even threatened to sue him while she never really had the guts to leave him. She was sure he loved her and that their love really was enough to make him change. So, as soon as he landed his big job with an oil servicing firm, he took her for a weekend getaway to Obudu Cattle ranch in Calabar and proposed to her. She said yes. After several beatings, two miscarriages and a broken spirit, she knew she should have said no.

She recalled coming back from the trip to Obudu and sharing the news of her engagement with her friends. 'Kome proposed!' She said to her closest friend, Yewande, as soon as she could call. Yewande didn't sound enthusiastic over the phone, and she showed even less enthusiasm when she saw her. She had witnessed Kome's violence first hand and thought Ainehi was making a mistake. But she didn't want to say that over the phone. 'I will see you at home this evening,' she said curtly. All that everyone talked about was how lovely the emerald cut engagement ring was. No one said a word about Kome, or how he proposed. Family members and friends thought Kome was toxic, but no one advised Kome to tread the pathway of their relationship with watchfulness.

Yewande showed up in the house that evening but without a smile on her face. "Ainehi, what on earth are you doing?" She asked with as much self-control as she could muster. 'I don't understand how you are fast becoming one of those women we talk about, helpless and so blinded by love that they end up ruinimg their own lives. "Kome has been nothing but poison since you guys met. How can you possibly think marrying him is a good idea when dating him is the dumbest thing I have ever seen you do?"

Ainehi felt the doubt in her heart even while she talked about the engagement. She had it while she planned the wedding but still craved Yewande's support and it was frustrating that she couldn't be happy for her scream at the sight of the lovely ring and asked what colours she would wear as her maid of honour. It didn't look like Yewande wanted to be at the wedding at all.

'Yewande, you don't understand how Kome and I feel about each other. He is a passionate person and sometimes that passion pushes him to act violently. But I know he loves me; he truly does,' Ainehi was desperate for having Yewande's support. She needed someone to tell her the doubts; she had meant nothing, and Yewande was not helping at all. "Can you even hear yourself? If I didn't know better, I would say he cast a spell on you." she started again ' you are flashing an engagement ring from a guy who almost killed you the last time he beat you up and left you alone. He brought you flowers the next day, flowers he would have placed on your grave if I hadn't shown up when you called.' She stood up and picked up her phone, "I need to call your mother to talk some sense into you…or maybe I should call your pastor instead so they can deliver you from this madness."

"Don't call my mum or anyone." Ainehi said angrily. "I have had enough of your jealousy. You always attack Kome and fail to see his good side. What do you know about being in a relationship? When was the last time you had one?' Ainehi knew she was hitting below the belt, but she wanted to hurt Yewande who had been off relationships for a while now. It was not a nice thing to say and she knew it. She wondered why they were fighting. They had been friends for over fifteen years, and this was certainly not how she pictured this scene in her head.

"I wish you and you fiancé good luck." Yewande said quietly as she picked up her bag and walked to the door. Then she paused, "I know you did not mean those mean things you said, and I know you are hoping Kome will change; but trust me, Ainehi, he won't. Like you always said when you were still thinking straight, people never truly change.'

No one who knew about her turbulent relationship with Kome was in support of the engagement. Her parents refused to give their blessings initially but only agreed reluctantly after Kome and his folks had come to assure them that he would behave himself. The date was set. The wedding was grand and all went well for a few months. Even Yewande was beginning to warm up to the new Kome. Ainehi was pregnant barely three months after and an ecstatic Kome started shopping for baby wares on every trip.

Ainehi was so certain the fairy tale would never end till the second trimester when she talked to Kome about hiring a nanny as soon as the baby was born so she could go back to work. But Kome flared up. 'What kind of irresponsible mother leaves her child alone with a nanny and goes to work?' He screamed. "Don't I provide enough for us? Why do you have to go back to work?" He asked.

"Kome, we always agreed I would work,' she retorted. 'How was I to know you would not use your head on this one? Okay, now I am spelling it out, you WILL NOT work while the kids are young,"he said with such infuriating finality to his voice.

"Did I ever tell you I wanted to be a full time housewife? How dare you plan turning me into one without my consent?" She lashed back at him but Kome laughed sarcastically.

"My darling, I do not need your consent. In this house, I am the alpha and omega." He declared.

"In your small-minded world, probably." She responded angrily.

Kome got really upset and slapped her. Maybe the pregnancy hormones gave her the guts, or probably her not being beaten for several months made her forget Kome's temper. Whichever it was, she lashed at him and cursed him out for hitting her. An enraged Kome hit her and pushed her down the stairs. Following her emergency visit to the hospital, it was confirmed that she had had miscarriage as result of her falling down. She packed a few of her things amidst several pleas from Kome and went to Yewande's.

Yewande knew better than to say, "I told you so." She was silent and supportive. "You need to tell both families." She said.

"I can't tell my folks, Yewande. I can't stand the I-told-you. It's barely eight months!" Ainehi said in disbelief "What kind of monster hits his pregnant wife?" She asked no one in particular. The same kind of monster who hit his girlfriend for three years, Yewande thought but said nothing. She thought of her boyfriend, Dimeji, and how many times she had wished there was more passion in her relationship. Looking at a bruised and broken Ainehi made her love docile Dimeji even more.

"So what will you tell everyone when they notice you are not getting bigger?" Yewande asked. "I know this is a lot for you to process right now dearie; but you cannot hide a pregnancy."

Ainehi started sobbing afresh "What have I got myself into?" She asked softly. 'I thought he would change with marriage and a baby coming. Kome had been over the moon with excitement since the pregnancy. He had started shopping already. Why did he have to kill our baby?' Yewande hugged her and let her cry it out. She knew in her heart that Ainehi would go back to Kome, just like she always did back in school. That was the sad reality. Theirs was a love that made no sense. Kome treated Ainehi like a queen when he was in his right frame of mind, but when the rage took over, the transformation was alarming. Kome was the poster boy for

Jekyll and Hyde. The doorbell buzzed; before Yewande could get up from the sofa, it buzzed again impatiently. By instinct, she knew it was Kome.

She walked angrily to the door, ready to give him a piece of her mind, and if things got ugly her dumb bells would come to her rescue. She was no Ainehi, blinded by love or some strange obsession; she would hit him if she had to. As she opened the door she eyed her dumbbells resting behind it with her exercise mat.

'Yewande please, I know Ainehi is here, I need to speak with her,' he said with so much pain in his eyes. Yewande almost cracked in sympathy. But the thought of Ainehi crying, and the loss of her potential god-child hardened her heart. "She is here, but I will not let her see you." she blurted. "What more do you want from her? You killed your own child, Kome? When will this end, when Ainehi gets killed by your rage?" He was sobbing quietly; his voice was so low that it was barely audible.

"I know I will never be able to forgive myself for this, but I need to speak with her. I need to explain. You don't need to explain anything; you need to apologise to her and pray God forgives you. Please, leave my house Kome." She said and shut the door.

Yewande walked back to the room where her friend was still huddled in a corner.

"That was Kome, he wanted to see you" She informed Ainehi. "I heard your conversation." Ainehi said.

"You were a bit too hard on him." Yewande retorted.

"What did you want me to do? Hug, console and invite him in for a drink." Ainehi asked, alarmed.

"I am not saying that, he sounded broken already and you just told him." Yewande cut in.

"If you were a child, I would spank you thoroughly. Wetin dey do you?" She inquired, quite angrily "Very soon, you will tell me you have to go back to the house." She looked at Ainehi who quickly looked away. "Oh, my goodness! You are considering going back already. That's why you can't even look me in the eyes!"

"He is still my husband, I can't just give up on my marriage that is not even up to a year." Ainehi explained in frustration "Ainehi! You want this guy to kill you abi?" Yewande was bewildered "I will not say anything about this to you anymore. As I can see, you don't think clearly. I will call your mum; maybe she can talk some sense to you." Three days later Ainehi was back with Kome.

This all happened two years ago and she had stayed. She had drowned herself in her work and enjoyed the marriage only when Kome was not enraged. She never knew when to expect an outburst; it was ever so random. He had given her a black eye and called her a whore because she had referred to Joe Manganiello as hot when watching Magic Mike. At the Ikeja Mall, he had shoved her roughly into the car, embarrassing her in front of her old classmate because, according to him, she had been very flirty when she was talking to him. He didn't allow her to attend an office dinner because he thought her dinner dress was slutty and did not portray her as a responsibly married woman. The list was endless. She had stayed on for two years, praying and hoping he would change. But he hadn't. Her hand went to her tummy, and she spoke softly to the child growing in the womb, 'I am so sorry I can't let you grow up knowing your father as a monster.' She sobbed softly.

She had been to the hospital that morning and the doctor had confirmed that she was pregnant. He had looked at her and said quietly, "Ainehi, I know this is none of my business…" He started, but she cut him short calmly. 'Then don't say anything doctor.' She stood up to leave. She could feel him looking at her sadly; maybe he wasn't sad and just thought her foolish. She knew what she had to do. Her gynaecologist, Dr. Solanke, was an experienced specialist. He was old but very supportive. He had seen her lose her first two pregnancies and he had his suspicion of how she lost the babies. Nevertheless, she never confirmed them. He had complained that her injuries and bruises were not consistent with her story. But she had to stick to it. He had seen her flinch when Kome tried to console her, and how they barely said anything to each other when the doctor addressed them in her recovery room. Kome's guilt filled the room like an independent presence, and the doctor was no fool. He knew Kome had abused her and that had led to the loss of the baby. She was too weak and embarrassed to say anything.

This time was different. She called Yewande on her way home.

"Hello Yewande, can you come over to the house this evening?"

"Sure girl, is anything up? Are you okay?" Yewande asked in apprehension, but Ainehi's voice was calm. The few words seemed to hold a lot. 'I am pregnant' she said in the same calm tone. "I am leaving Kome." Yewande was ecstatic but she remained calm. This was the first time Ainehi had mentioned leaving Kome, and from the tone of her voice, she knew she was serious. "I will be there as soon as I can get out of the office. Ainehi, please don't call Kome till I come over." Yewande said in a pleading tone. The last thing she needed was Kome's convincing her to stay.

Ainehi laughed humourlessly. "Yewande, you know me better than anyone. I might forever decide, but when I do…" she stopped abruptly. Ainehi went home and sat down, thinking of her last two pregnancies and how she had stupidly failed her last two babies by

staying with Kome. She was done making mistakes. She wanted to cut her losses and start all over. She was going to have her baby, and file for a divorce afterwards. Being a lawyer had its perks; she knew what she had to do.

It started drizzling and it felt good hearing the rain drops on the roof. It felt like nature was bringing rhythm into her thoughts.

77

Yewande would be over soon, and Ainehi wanted her to help her pack and take some of her things in her car. She would move the rest later. She just didn't want any confrontation with Kome, and moving her things would make her have fewer reasons to hang around. She had packed her certificates and other vital documents in her small carryon. She moved her jewellery case and other smaller valuables into the same carryon and kept them aside. Her clothes and shoes were shoved into huge travel boxes. She didn't bother folding them neatly. It wasn't really necessary. She could hear the rain getting heavier and she knew the electricity would go off soon. It always did when it rained. Either the power company would turn it off, or, in some cases, the storm would cause some major electrical fault and they would be stuck with the noisy generators. She kept packing and with each suitcase closed, she felt a step closer to freedom. She could smell it like the dust raised by the rainfall. Ainehi dragged the suitcases to the main entrance and was preparing dinner when Yewande came.

"This rain makes you feel like there is a Noah somewhere in an Ark and we did not get the memo." Yewande attempted a joke as she rushed inside, dumping her brolly by the door. She stopped in her tracks when she saw the already packed suitcases. "You are doing this?" Yewande asked her, still stunned.

"Now, or never." Ainehi responded "it's about time." Yewande hugged her and asked.

"Have you told your folks yet?"

"No, I will call them when I am at yours. You know I have to stay at yours till I figure this out." Ainehi said, pouting innocently. They both laughed.

"You know you don't need to make the puss-in-boots face for this. Mi casa es su casa." Yewande added in her phony Spanish accent.

"Thanks dear, I will get the mai guard to help with the luggage. Just carry these; I will bring the others tomorrow."

"Are you sure you should stay over alone with Kome tonight? What if he gets violent knowing you are about to leave?" Yewande was visibly worried. "I think we should leave and you can ask him to meet you somewhere public."

"No. I have to do this for closure. I will not lose another child because of Kome and his rage. I need to talk to him tonight'." Yewande tried to convince her, but she insisted on waiting.

It was 8pm when Yewande left and she prepared dinner as usual. She sat down to watch TV for a bit but could not concentrate. Then she sat by the window, watching the downpour. The window overlooked the balcony, the same balcony from which Kome had pushed her almost a year ago. She shivered at the thought of it all. She had blanked out for a few months, and that was when she lost the second baby. Her hand went to her stomach protectively. She stood up abruptly and called the mai guard again.

"Musa, take the boxes in my room to the car." She ordered.

"Madam,you dey travel?" Musa asked, looking at her curiously.

"Yes...no...just take them to the car please." She said, not really sure what to say to Musa.

She picked up her pen. She wanted to pour out her heart in the letter, but she was too scared that he would come home and find her packing. What was she thinking of waiting to confront him with the news of her pregnancy and leaving him at same time. Yewande was right; it didn't make any sense at all as there was no predicting Kome's reaction. He didn't even sound like he was in a good mood when he told her not to wait up. Well, she would do him one better; she would not be here at all.

Closure was exaggerated. Whatever she had to say she would do it in front of their families and a lawyer. She was done.

She left him a note.

Diary of a Wedding Planner

They say marriages are made in Heaven, but so is Thunder and Lightening

- Clint Eastwood

S

he went on and on, saying the same thing the exact same way over and over! I might as well put her on replay. I guessed she never heard the word rephrase.

I was so bored and it took a lot to keep me from screaming. I kept telling myself: "She is your boss and she has your pay cheque." I said this over and over in my head like a mantra. Then, the phone rang. Her phone. Thank goodness! We had to put an end to the meeting that had lasted way over three hours! That was one of our nose-in-the-air, old money clients in Ikoyi.

At the other end of the table, poised, elegant and as cold as ice, sat my managing partner, Morenike. Renike reminded me of those beautiful, cold, vicious, Russian KGB Mossad-Bond girl type in the movies or, for fans of the series, Legend of the Seeker, the Mord Sith. She was a cross between those mean little fishes, piranhas, from South America waters and a graceful eagle. Don't ask me how. My imagination could be warped at times.

A few hours after Mrs. Derin Campbell whom I called our oldmoney client had gone, a delivery guy walked in from my favourite pizza parlour, Debonair. He had called earlier to confirm a delivery for Izehi. I thought that was strange because I could not remember ordering a pizza. So I asked: "Are you sure?" To prove how sure he was, he quoted my mobile number. Still surprised, I drilled him a bit more.

"What's the name of the person who placed the order?"

"Madam, he didn't leave his name. He just paid and said we should take it to you."

Enough with questions. I quickly grabbed it, said thank you and asked Renike to join in the surprise feast lest we were told it was a mistake and the package withdrawn. I was still curious about the sender though. Renike was usually the one who got anonymous gifts.

I looked at my watch. It was 3pm. Asides the pizza, it had been one crazy day. Client service could be fun and exciting but it could also try your patience as a manager in an establishment that handled women and all the crazy, frenzy stuff of wedding planning. I also doubled, reluctantly though, as a marriage counsellor! People found it easy to confide in me. This maybe because I didn't have the heart to call their bluff on all the bulls**ts. So I listened to reluctant brides, happy brides, bitchy brides and any other type that came my way. By any other type, I mean pushy mothers, nosy mothers-in-law, crazy friends, jealous friends and any of the female species that walked in, not forgetting the impatient groom who, in most cases, hated being at the wedding planners' but had been forced by their brides.

It's a crazy world in our business and for someone who was cynical about all things marriage, I must say Renike did an excellent job. She and I were as different as night and day in personality but physically we could pass for twins. I being the nice one and she, the wicked witch of the West a la Wizard of Oz.

I thought Renike loved me being with her despite the fact that she thought I was too soft (which in a strange way was also my selling point). I kept the customers with my charm and sweetness while she satisfied them with her excellent planning skills.

I grew up in Nigeria. She went to one of those fancy Swiss finishing schools and had experienced the glitz and glamour of Paris before deciding to bring all that glitz to the Nigerian wedding industry. That was how she put it.

This is how I met Renike, and how this all started…

Renike and I met three years ago at a friend's Christmas party. She was one of those people who walked into a room and you could not help but notice. Flawless skin, graceful mien and an aura that reeked of an almost intimidating confidence. I was there with another friend and from afar, we watched as some wimpy guy, who was totally smitten by her, drooled. To woo a girl like Renike, you had to be confident.

Some hours later, I heard her husky voice behind me. "You must be Izehi," she said.

It didn't sound like a question, so I just smiled.

She went on: "I figured it had to be you. I have heard all night people saying we could pass for twins." She gave me a sweeping look. A look that seemed to say, "You are the ugly twin."

I was very irritated. I knew I didn't take as much care with details as she did. I was not into all the elegant details. I was a lot simpler. I was beautiful…but Renike, gorgeous! I decided there and then not to like her. Just when I was going to excuse myself and walk away, an acquaintance of mine walked up to me and she was whining about her forthcoming wedding and how it would be great if she could get a wedding planner she could trust with all the details.

Before I could respond, I heard: "Izehi and I can handle it."

I turned to see Renike stretch out her hands, introduce herself as my friend who was into events and weddings, and the like. She painted a picture of a fairy-tale wedding there and then, and voila! we had our first wedding to plan.

It was crazy. I was furious. What the heck was she talking about? I hated events. I barely attended, much less plan. Beside that, I disliked Renike and her pushy, cocky, arrogant self. But on the other hand, I was intrigued. I was slightly excited and fascinated, which made me turn and glared at her.

She said, "Trust me. This will work like a charm."

It did and I never had a cause to look back. The business was actually owned by Renike. I was more of a junior partner because the money and the ideas were actually hers. She always joked I was the sanity in the partnership; I kept her from strangling annoying clients. Ours was a ying-yang type of relationship. She came from old money and I from no-money. By old money I mean those born wealthy and with all the privileges. So, she was never intimidated by the arrogant rich because it was the world she grew up in. I must admit I got intimidated sometimes.

The nouveau riche (new money) were the best clients to deal with. Those who had made some serious money legally or illegally. They always felt they had something to prove. So they spent crazy on fashion, trying to prove that they had arrived. Yet, they lacked the aristocratic confidence of the old moneybags.

We grouped our clients, mentally, into two categories: Lekki, new money fellows; and Ikoyi, the real blue blood. We got away with our pretty faces and suave charisma. Renike did not go to a Swiss finishing school just for nothing! She made weddings into fairy-tales!

I studied French. Renike once lived in Paris. So, we threw in the razzmattazz that made us classier and elitist. Something the nouveau riche fell for all the time, and for which we billed them heavily. During meetings with our clients, we would throw in a few French phrases here and there. We mentioned Bordeux a lot with the wine details. Mentioned hors d'oevres when planning the meals. Talked about haute couture and casually dropped French terms like joie de vivre, de javu and savoir faire. There was something about French that simply screamed class without even trying.

Back to our boring, snotty client. She went on and on about how she had attended a wedding in England and the theme was all white and snowy. Snowy! How the heck were we supposed to make that happen? White and crystals could make a place look heavenly and dreamy but she went on and on about the snowy look.

At some point, I could tell Renike was no longer there mentally. She was so bored it showed. I was the nice one. So I had to keep an interested look while she yapped away, and I did the whole "She's your boss; she holds your pay cheque" mantra. Thinking of clients as bosses helped me tolerate them.

As soon as she left, just before my mystery pizza delivery, Renike yelled: "Can you believe the old hag? Her daughter isn't even here. She came ahead of her daughter, the bride, to come tell us what she wanted! Who does that?"

When hysterical or upset, her usually husky voice got high-pitched and a bit shrilly. I smiled and said, "You are the wedding miracle worker. Do your thing, girl."

"I can't make a snowy look. She will just have to make do with lots of white and soft-textured fabrics."

I could almost hear the wheels in her brain working it out. She loved the challenge. She would make it so damn good the lady would think she was in the North Pole. I knew how to work on her ego. I made her feel she could pull through anything. Truth be told, she could pull through almost anything. As we were trying to figure out the detail, he walked in. But that's a different story.

You know how it was with some people? They walked into a room and the entire room became a stage. They became stars. That was Kene. The minute he walked into our office, I had two things going on in my head simultaneously.

First, I had Norah Jones' Come Away with me playing in my head. Second, I wished Renike would suddenly disappear or at least step into the inner office.

The first thought was because Kene was exactly the type of guy you actually think of running away with. He was about 6'3" with perfect dark chocolate skin; eyes that seemed to squint and see through your very soul and a smile that had this cynicism that was damn right attractive. The second thought was because I felt plain beside Renike and if he were like most men, he would be hitting on her pretty soon.

Don't get me wrong, I have more than my fair share of admirers but when with Renike, I always felt like I was second choice or a consolation price for the schmucks who didn't have the guts to step up to her. I was secretly hoping this extremely good-looking guy would have a flaw somewhere. Then he spoke and all I could say in my head was 'Thank God, I am sitting down' because I couldn't feel my legs anymore. His voice was deep and calm at the same time. Like he could hypnotize you just by talking.

"You ladies must be the wedding planners right?" He addressed both of us but was walking towards Renike.

Okay, to be fair to him, she was closer to the entrance. So it was only logical that he'd walk towards her, not me.

"I am in a bit of a rush. I only have a few minutes as I have a flight in two hours," he continued.

"Yes we are, but we are going to need more than a few minutes if you are going to plan a wedding," Renike said, standing up to attend to him. "I am Renike and that's my partner, Izehi."

I could not exactly trust myself to speak, so I nodded and smiled my hello from the end of the room.

"I am not the one getting married," he said. "I promised my sister I would stop by to make an appointment for her before heading to the airport. That's why I am here."

Renike's face lit up in an enthusiastic smile. "Oh! Then just fill out this slip and, voila! your sister has an appointment," she quipped.

Renike never gets all fluttery nor quippy. The smile told me a lot; she was just as smitten by him as I was. But she was calm enough to handle it better.

"So you are travelling, you live outside Lagos?" She continued while he filled out the form. Renike flirted and I stared stupidly in a corner.

"I live here in Lagos but I fly a lot. I am a pilot," he said, not taking his eyes off the form as he scribbled his sister's detail. Then he looked up and caught me staring. I felt like killing myself! "Izehi right? You remind me of a friend of mine, Nosa. We were in the same department in Uni."

As he spoke, he walked closer to me. Then he mentioned Raymond's last name and I finally found my voice.

"He is my cousin, same last name." I explained in a voice that sounded alien to me.

"The resemblance is uncanny!" He exclaimed. "The difference is you are definitely better looking. Nosa never told us he had a beauty queen for a cousin," he teased.

I must have blushed all shades of red. Here I was, a full grown Lagos Island big girl, blushing like a teenager over a mere compliment. "Her appointment is for 11am," Renike interjected.

My guess was she wasn't liking the tone of our conversation, and the fact that I was stealing the spotlight away from her, was definitely not her idea of fun.

"Do ask her to inform us if she will not be able to make that time, so we can reschedule," her voice was no longer sweet and flirty but succinctly polite and officious.

"Will do," Kene said. "Here's my card. Please ask Nosa to give me a call. It will be really nice to hear from him again," he said looking me straight in the eyes.

Something told me the card was meant for me, and Nosa was simply a decoy. Maybe I was right or maybe I was paying too much attention to the butterflies fluttering in my stomach.

As soon as Kene left, there was a certain unease in our office. Renike's look softened and she smiled at me. It was obvious we were both thinking about my ex-fiancé, Tayo. It had been almost three years.

Tayo was Renike's cousin whom she had introduced to me and we had hit it off and started dating barely two months after we met. Renike initially did not like the idea but later encouraged us when she saw that being in love did not slow me down at work. Yes, I fell head over heels in love with Tayo; one of my biggest regrets till date.

Tayo was very intelligent, business-savvy and street-smart. He was as charming as he was good-looking. He could talk a monkey into parting with its bananas. These paid off in business. He was successful but not much of his success could be attributed to his oil magnate father. He was an astute businessman.

Tayo also had more scandals than any one man should. When it came to the opposite sex, it was safe to say his brain was located elsewhere. Did you catch my drift? Two divorces at thirty-nine should have given me a clue but the heart could be obstinate and I kept telling myself he was much younger then.

If scandals had in no way slowed him down, not even age could do that. Renike detested that he just couldn't keep it in his pants. With more money than they could spend, he was used to getting his way in general and with women in particular. From the minute Renike introduced us, I became his mark.

We had just registered RED – Rubies, Emeralds and Diamonds – and were pitching to our third client. He was Tayo's friend and as his contribution to the wedding, he had offered to hire a professional wedding planner. So he decided to hire us to plan the wedding. As a rule, when it came to family and friends, we always allowed the other handle business. Tayo being Renike's family, the lot fell on me to handle the financial details. This meant talking to her cousin sometimes and ultimately picking up our cheque from his place.

I had met Tayo at functions a number of times before and he knew me as Renike's business partner. On several occasions, he had asked me out but I had always declined till now that this business made us interact a lot more than ever. Going to his office to get a cheque did not seem like a big deal. But on getting there, from the hostile reception I got from his secretary (I can bet my partnership at RED, that he had slept with and was probably still sleeping with her) and from the gist I heard about Tayo, his escapades and his famous generosity to his women, I started thinking maybe coming here was a mistake. But then I thought, I was just picking up a cheque. What's the worst that could happen?

I waited for a while. He was in a meeting and had some other people waiting to see him. He finished with them and even attended to those who came after me. I was getting really upset. I hated being kept at the reception like I was coming there to collect an allowance from a sugar daddy. Eventually, he despatched them all and asked me to come in.

"Sorry to have kept you waiting, Izehi," he gushed, giving me a hug that was far from being brotherly. "Have you had lunch? I am famished."

"Not yet, but I…" I tried to say I would have lunch at the office but he interrupted.

"Then you must join me for lunch. I am just about to head for REEDS on Awolowo Road."

I looked at my Cartier. It was almost 4pm. I was actually hungry, so I said okay. We got to the car park. Tayo insisted that there was no point taking my car. After lunch, we would come back to his office and I could pick my car. It made sense because my office was on the opposite side, which meant I would still have to drive down that way anyway. With the fuel scarcity in town, why waste the precious commodity?

I figured he would give me the cheque after lunch but as we approached Falomo Bridge from Victoria Island, he asked the driver to head straight to a place that sounded more like a guest house somewhere on Osborne.

"I thought we were going to REEDS on Awolowo Road. Staying on the bridge means we are heading towards Kingsway," I observed. He just smiled and said, "I know a better place. It's very private and really comfortable."

As he said those words: private and comfortable, I could detect from the undertone and that ever familiar glint in the eyes of a man when all he could think of was how to get to the fastest place for a quick fix that he was being mischievous.

According to my friend, Renike, a man with a hard-on is like a junkie in need of a fix. Well, Tayo proved Renike and I wrong that day. He drove to his house and made lunch. It was his special fried Indomie noodles and a week later, we became an item.

Renike did not like it one bit. She knew it would not end well. This caused a strain in our business for the three months I stupidly dated Tayo. Several messy scandals in blogs and tabloids later, and I knew Tayo was definitely Mr. Wrong.

I could have sworn that the new client or rather potential client who had just walked in and eased the tension between Renike and I could not afford our services. She had the dishevelled look of someone who had lived a tough life. Her skin seemed a bit sallow and wrinkled. She was most likely in her late sixties but looked like someone in her hundreds!

I could tell from the snotty look on Renike's face that she was not amused. She usually left the charity cases as we dubbed them to me. I was the people- person. So whenever we had people who wanted a million-dollar services for a hundred, Renike haughtily let me handle them.

"Good afternoon, Ma'am." I managed a smile. "Who is getting married?" I asked heartily.

Her response was every event planners dream. "My only granddaughter," she said with so much warmth. "And we are not sparing any cost," she added with the excitement of a child.

The minute Renike heard those magic words that symbolized a blank cheque, she became a lot nicer and joined in on the conversation. "She is such a lucky bride," she said in her sweetest voice, a voice she reserved for the three Fs – family, friends and fat cheques!

When I talk about Renike, it's not that I hated her. It's almost impossible to hate her. You might be angry, jealous, upset, want to strangulate her sometimes, but you also had to admire and respect her for so many reasons. Renike was the kind of girl you love to hate and hate to love. She was an enigma.

One could rarely deceive the old folks. They weren't called old folks for nothing. They knew all the tricks in the book. So Mrs. A was not fooled by Renike's charms. She knew she was speaking to her because she had said they were willing to spend an amount.

"I will be here with my granddaughter tomorrow. I just wanted to be sure you could do hers for the said date," she continued. "She has some strange colours and ideas in mind. I don't have the detail but I am sure they will make sense to you young ladies." I smiled in agreement.

"Whatever she wants, we can deliver." Renike cut in. "I believe you must have...."

"Like I was saying...," Mrs. A continued as if Renike hadn't even spoken. "I am quite sure you ladies will understand and make it as perfect as she would want it. I saw the wedding you planned for the Kadiris last month; a very tasteful ceremony I must admit."

As she spoke, I smiled at intervals and did what anybody in my shoes would do. She was talking big, so I was accessing her to see if she seemed just as big. I was no jewellery expert. She wore a simple gold earring, an emerald cut ring, set in what seemed like white gold (possibly platinum) and she had on a Patek Philippe ladies' chronograph watch!

OK. I had to scream about the watch. I loved watches, and Patek Philippe watches didn't come cheap. This particular watch cost over $60,000 the last time I checked.

While I assess her, Renike walked towards the window sulking. I could tell she wanted to see what car Mrs. A had come in. It was all part of the 'verifying her status' process. After all, the ring might not be emerald and the Patek might be fake! Renike and I locked gaze and I knew whatever the ride was, she was extremely impressed because she was beaming all over.

Mrs. A stood up to leave and I stood up to walk her to the door.

"Thank you for stopping by, Ma'am." I was beaming too, because I was so sure we had hit the jackpot. "We'll see you at 12 noon tomorrow."

Then she said, "Could we make it 11am instead? I have a meeting to attend at 1pm, and I know these things take time."

At the back of my mind I remembered we had the appointment with our pilot guy's sister for tomorrow but what the hell? I could call them to reschedule for earlier or later. We could smell the money on Mrs A. I heard myself say, "Not a problem at all, Ma. 11am will be perfect."

As she walked out of the door, Renike screamed. "She came in a Rolls Royce Phantom!"

When it came to money and business, men and all their drama always took a back seat for Renike and I. The excitement at the prospect of a blank cheque was enough to make us forget our pilot crush. At least for now.

Kene was definitely a forgotten topic as I could almost see the creative wheels, churning out ideas in the factory that was Renike's mind. I knew she was going to be very quiet for the next couple of minutes dreaming up amazing ideas and after that, she was going to bombard me with the detail. It would then be my turn to piece them together.

Renike and I made an awesome team. I had started dialling to find out which of the large venues could be secured for the wedding. Usually, we loved working with large venues like Landmark in Victoria Island Annexe because it was spacious and you could do almost anything with it. You could create unbelievable themes as long as the client was ready to dole out the cash.

"I was thinking," Renike said, "we have kinda used Landmark as a venue for too long. There is this new place, the one Ofure had her wedding in in Ikoyi. Maybe we could try securing it." I had no clue what venue she was talking about.

"I wasn't at Ofure's wedding, Renike. It was same weekend I had to travel for my Aunt M's funeral, remember?"

I had lost a very dear aunt around that period and had to leave Renike to handle the client alone. She was so frustrated, having to deal with Ofure's tantrums. Ofure happened to be our dear friend but one of those very dramatic people who always saw a million ways things could go wrong.

The wedding was a huge success but Renike wouldn't speak to Ofure for an entire week after it, saying she could strangle her just to get even.
"Well, Ize, you might have to call Ofure or we could drive down there together."

It was always better to see the place and visualize. Personally, I would rather see the place bare of decorations. I felt it helped you build your own ideas without the distraction of the decorations.

"Works for me," I said. I knew my next sentence would set Renike off but it had to be said. "I know you hate to hear this, but we have to let Ify in on this deal."

As I uttered the statement, I had already envisaged Renike's reaction.

"What the hell for?" She hissed.

Ify was a superb cake craftswoman. One of those who could create anything you wanted with fondant and you would have no reason to fret. But, according to Renike, Ify was just an overpriced cow, who had no respect for business etiquette.

Yes, we both agreed her services were anything but cheap. I reckoned it was not our money. When dealing with moneybags, I knew what would sell.

Ify was bi-racial. She learnt how to make gateaux from some of the experts in France. We also had Glen, a white female photographer. Not because she was better than the legendary Sumi Smart-Cole or TY Bello but because Nigerians would pay us more if they saw a Caucasian. So we exploited that weakness shamelessly.

Renike could not stand Ify. They had their differences way back from school days in Paris. They had a history, a story of rivalry that they never talked about. I knew they could put their differences aside for the sake of business. They had done so before. Why not now?

Old-money's wedding was successfully executed, with Renike and Ify staying completely out of each other's way and yours truly being the intermediary all through the event.

We were so comfortable with our pot of gold that we decided it was time we put our feet up and relax. Renike and I never travelled at same time, as the business needed at least one of us to interface with clients whenever either had to be excused from work. So, Renike took off for two weeks while I held down the fort. Our calendar always determined our vacations.

She called on a Saturday announcing her arrival. So it was no surprise seeing her at work on Monday morning.

"So, who pays for the next vacation?" was the first thing she said as she walked in.

That was her usual line after spending too much money. When she goes on a shopping spree, she would ask, "So who is paying for all these items?" It was our way of saying a new client had to come in to fill the financial void such splurging had created.

"Buon giorno bella," I said playfully, laughing at my poor Italian accent.

She gave a quick hug and shoved a shopping bag at me.

"Finally, you can stop ogling this online," she said.

Renike's taste was exquisite and her gifts had a way of always reminding you her taste.

"Awwwww, that's so sweet. What did you get me?" I asked, digging into the gift bag.

When I pulled out the box and beheld its content, I was left speechless.

"Oh My God! Where on earth did you find this?" My voice was quaking with emotion. It was a very rare antique-styled Panerai Luminor wristwatch I had seen online, and I had mentioned that it looked like a collector's piece. But it was sold out. I had no idea Renike even noticed how much I wanted it.

"Now, don't get all mushy on me," she said jocularly. "It wasn't like I went searching all over Milan for it. I bumped into it and thought, what the hell! It has been a good year for us." Then she added, "I have to say this Ize; for the price I paid for that piece, you are certainly not getting a birthday or a Christmas gift for the next two years! Those silly watches are frigging expensive!"

I was so touched, I ran to give her a bear hug. I was not supposed to expect a gift for the next 5years because these watches cost as much as $4,000! With my obsession over watches, it was a surprise I still wouldn't even buy one of these expensive stuff for myself!

But that was Renike; unpredictably sweet one minute and a Mord Sith the next.

Her gift was a sign of better things to come. Two days later, a promotional first-class ticket in hand, hair perfectly done, my smile wider than Julia Roberts' and my heart filled with thoughts of the sea and the sun, then I saw him. Still as drop-dead-gorgeous as the day he walked into our office a few months ago. He walked in with the other members of the flight crew and said, "Well, well...if it isn't Nosa's cousin..."

That was how it all started.

"Hello, ermmmm…" Here was I, really excited to see him and still mumu enough to pretend to have forgotten the name.

"Kene," he said quickly and went, "Wow! Great seeing you again. You guys refused to plan my sister's wedding, abi?" he said rhetorically.

"I really do apologise but it clashed with another wedding we were already contracted to plan."

Of course, my explanation was not entirely true. His sister's wedding was to hold the weekend before moneybag's wedding. Planning, as we already knew would be intense for the latter. So, we weighed our options, and being true business women that we were, we went for the money.

"Listen gorgeous, we had someone ready to pay us twice as much as your sister would have paid us. So we dropped her like a boiling kettle!"

Okay, I did not say this out loud, just in my head. I said instead, "We did explain to your sister why we couldn't plan her wedding and recommended someone we knew could handle it just as well." I tried to explain lamely.

Truth be told, Renike and I prided ourselves as the best in Lagos.

"I hope it was a beautiful ceremony?' I asked.

"It certainly was, though she still felt you guys would have done better."

Smart woman, I said in my mind.

"Where are you headed?" he asked while stopping to rummage through his carry-on for what turned out to be another mobile phone. "My crew and I are doing a charter to Greece. We will be there for a week."

"Are you kidding me? I am going to Greece too! Actually, I am doing a few stops: Venice, Athens, Paris, but starting with London. I promised my sister I would spend a few days with her in London before starting the vacation proper."

The day just kept getting better. He turned to his colleagues.

"I really have to run. We have to do a briefing before the flight." He said as he gestured to his colleagues. "Can I have your London contact? I will call to see if we can have drinks or see the sites in Greece together," he said to me.

Numbers exchanged, we parted ways while I went to check in at the Virgin Atlantic counter. I knew the stay at my sister's in London was going to be cut short because now, more than ever, I was looking forward to getting to Greece and having a little bit of Kene.

Next stop after London was meant to be Paris. Not anymore. I called my travel agent. We had some rescheduling to do.

Norah Jones' Come away with me was playing somewhere or was it just my imagination?

The Applicant

I can't impress you with the cars and the wealth, 'cos any woman with WILL and DRIVE can get it herself.

- Sean 'Diddy' Combs

Osas hated spending Christmas in Benin but, unfortunately for her, she had to. It was Esohe's wedding and they had both grown up as thick as thieves, sharing similar experiences in their dormitory at Federal Government College, Benin. They had a lot in common; still did and had stayed friends over the past fifteen years.

They had both grown up without their parents. Esohe's dad left her with his mother in-law after his wife died giving birth to her. He paid her bills but there was no father-daughter relationship. Osas on the other hand knew both her parents and saw them at family gatherings sometimes. They had her out of wedlock and had moved on to other people. Both girls had bonded over similar backgrounds, growing up with doting and overbearing grandmothers. They were like sisters. Now that she was getting married, Osas was going to be the chief bridesmaid and there was no avoiding Benin.

She knew this trip was going to be hell for her. She was almost thirty, jobless, man-less and going for a wedding with a lot of family members in attendance. She could already hear Aunty Iziegbe asking, "So, when are we coming to eat your own rice?" That was her special way of saying "When are you getting married so we can fete with you?"

A more sympathetic Aunty Ifueko would chip in: "Don't worry, my dear, God's time is the best. Don't worry about it too much and at the same time, don't be too selective, men are all the same. Just make sure he has the money to take care of you and your family."

She should know men, Osas thought. Aunty Ifueko had been married three times and her houses in Lagos, Benin and Abuja were testaments to her good choices.

This was always how all family weddings she had attended in the last five years went, with the constant marriage talks. Now, more than ever, she felt insecure at the thought, considering her current state.

The mail alert on her phone startled her, bringing her back from her reverie. She had been checking her mail incessantly all week, hoping and praying for some positive news. The entire year had been one sob story or the other and she really needed this job, so seeing the name of the telecoms company she had interviewed with made her heart beat even faster.

Nervously, she clicked on the mail and the first line said it all: "We regret to inform you …."

Her spirit sank. She had read one too many of these emails and knew what it meant. She was still jobless.

Maybe she was cursed like her witch of a landlady told her two months ago when she asked for reimbursement after fixing a major electrical fault in her apartment. No husband, no job, no money! Just a handful of relationships that had led nowhere in the last five years she had lived in this apartment. Maybe the house was cursed. She laughed humourlessly at her own superstitious thought. She was not a bad girl. Just unfortunate in love, job, family and a few other things.

Another alert. She read the message on WhatsApp; it was her ex, Seyi. He kept sending her messages, telling her how miserable his marriage was and how he wishes he had married her even when his parents did not want an Omo Ibo. Osas was Bini, from Edo State. But to Seyi and his family, if you are not Hausa or Yoruba, then you are certainly Igbo. She deleted his messages. If he thought his pathetic lamentations made her feel special, then he was not as smart as she thought.

Osas had met Seyi's wife at a friend's wedding two years ago. She was pretty, a bit overweight though, she thought. Osas knew herself as gorgeous. She had a good mirror and had seen the looks of admiration on people's faces whenever she walked into a room. She was dark-skinned, tall and had a figure that would make many women jealous. She might not be every man's idea of beauty but she was certainly no one's idea of ugliness.

In a few months, she was going to be thirty. The milestone that would strip her of any security the twenties offered. She was a step closer to becoming an old maid if things did not happen soon. Then, the sad talks from family and friends as regards marriage would increase.

Her landlady and neighbours would look at her with pity and even disdain whenever she had any male visitor irrespective of his age or relationship with her. Her married neighbours would frown if their husbands said more than a good morning or smiled too much at her because they would see her as a potential husband snatcher, a thought she was sure they already nursed. Married female friends would find her uninteresting because she did not engage in baby talks, and she might be a potential husband snatcher if she was a little too chummy with their husbands. The husbands might have likely told their wives that she was a terrible influence because they heard her talking about her dates with them.

Some would stay in touch and after a few months of being married.

They became experts in all things men and bugged her with dating tips or introduced her to some man they met so that she could settle down. Work colleagues would stop inviting her to family events. It would not have mattered if only she had work colleagues. One had to hold down a job before one could have colleagues. Wouldn't one?

She had spoken with Dr. Dada against her better judgement. He had been one of the regular clients at her last job. He always talked about how smart she was and how he would like to poach her to come work in his firm. She had always hated the way he stared at her cleavage but after her company cut down its staff strength for financial reasons, she had taken her resume to his office. He told her he was busy and she should bring it to a hotel somewhere in Ikoyi later that evening so they could both go over it properly. Obviously he wanted to go over other things and she didn't, so she went back home with her resume.

She spoke with Alhaji Mukhtar. He sounded very willing to help. Even gave her a thousand dollars to help with some bills. Then came the punch line: he thought they could discuss her career better on his trip to Abu Dhabi. She took the money and declined the trip. He made it sound like the Abu Dhabi sun made her career prospect a lot brighter. They were all the same.

She thought about the six degrees of separation theory. Was it really a theory? She wondered how many degrees away from Dangote she was. A few millions would be quite useful, Uncle D. She laughed at the thought. Maybe being broke was driving her crazy. Yielding to Alhaji Muktar's proposition would have given her landlady something to talk about.

Osas knew she was neither lazy nor irresponsible. She had worked diligently since she was twenty-four, right after her National Youth Service Corps programme in Enugu State. Here she was, six years after: not enough experience for the high-profile jobs she applied for and too old for the available few fresh graduate jobs. It had been almost a year since the firm she worked with for the past four years downsized due to financial crisis. Now she was just a jobless Lagos girl, with depleted savings and unsure of her next rent.

She thought of Esohe getting married to the man of her dreams. She knew her parents would probably attend, as they knew Esohe's family well. Osas decided she would go see Iye as soon as she arrived in Benin before going to Esohe's house where she would have to stay. Iye was what she fondly called her grandmother. It meant mother, and her grandmother had been that and much more. She used to wonder why neither one of her parents wanted her but she had long made her peace with that.

She dragged herself out of bed and looked at the clock. It was 8:30am. She wore her running shoes and took them off. It was a bit too late to go running. She felt it would seem like announcing to the world she did not have a job. She decided to put off the morning run and do it at night instead.

She recalled reading a popular blog. Was it Linda Ikeji or Bella Naija? She read both blogs religiously these days, so she was unsure which one exactly had written about girls and guys who transported themselves from Ikorodu to come jog in Ikoyi. They would come in their form-hugging workout clothes, all in a bid to hoodwink some affluent Ikoyi residents. She thought this was absurd and laughed out loud.

She didn't believe in fairy-tales or happily-ever-afters. Life had not given her any reason to think of such happening to her. She was a Christian, had faith and believed God could do anything but she just wasn't holding her breath waiting for any favours. When she went jogging in her Maryland neighbourhood, all she thought of was the release running gave her. She needed the physical exertion, and as she once playfully told Esohe, it sharpened her resolve – the refusal to be single, jobless and fat. She loved her toned physique and had no intention of losing it to junk food and endless hours in front of cable TV.

She thought of her most persistent admirer, Chidi. He had been asking her out for ages. Maybe it's time she gave him a chance. Although they seemed as different as night was to day. He had asked her out on a movie date at The Palms in Lekki, then some music at Soul Lounge. She loved the old school vibe and it had been a while since she went out. She made a mental note: call and accept Chidi's dinner invitation. The last time they talked, she mentioned seeing a play at Terra Kulture and he said it wasn't his thing. She had invited him to a book reading at Bogobiri and he had a very bored look all through. So she had decided he was certainly not her type.

They had almost nothing in common aside chemistry. But these were desperate times. Good-looking, comfortable and well-spoken, they could work around hobbies and pastimes if things got serious, she thought.

Another mental note: she needed to call her former colleague, Nneoma. Nneoma had told her of a call-centre job opening at her

109

place of work and guaranteed her she could pull some strings to get her the job. The pay was just about a hundred grand. Initially she had turned down the job, but she was going to eat humble pie and accept it if it was still available. She yawned, just like the character in the documentary she was watching did.

She wondered why science, with all its purported research, could not explain simple coincidences like this. Why looking at someone yawning in reality or even on TV made one yawn, or why girls had synced menstrual cycle with other girls when they spend lots of time together like sisters, best friends, roommates and work colleagues! It seemed odd that there were no logical explanations for occurrences like these. She needed a job badly. Serious minded people were at their workplaces, and here she was forming expert researcher of all things mundane.

She called Nneoma.

"Hey girl! How you dey?" She asked casually.

"My dear, I dey o. We are inducting those new call-centre guys we just recruited," Nneoma responded, killing every hope Osas had for the job.

"Oh, that's cool," she replied. "I was going to stop by with your cookies but…"

"Babe, no buts, please. For those cookies of yours, I don't mind getting a query at work," she interrupted quickly.

Osas laughed. She knew all her friends loved her cookies. She used it to curry their favour whenever she needed one.

"When is your lunch break? I could easily walk down later." Nneoma's office was just two streets away from Osas' apartment block.

"1: 00pm. I will be available anytime from one. I have my yummy home- made smoothie to wash it down with nicely," she replied playfully. "See you later girl."

Osas hung up and checked her cookie jar. She hadn't called Nneoma to discuss cookies but she had to say something after she was told, in not so many words, that the job opening was gone, and all she could come up with was that. Now she had to take cookies to Nneoma.

She left her apartment at 1:15pm. She really didn't like visiting friends during work hours. When she did, she made the visits very brief. So, she figured she would be back on time to watch Husband for Hire on Telemundo at 2:30pm.

Nneoma took her to the office cafeteria where they shared her smoothie and ate cookies. Two of her colleagues joined in the cookie binge and the visit took a whole new turn.

"Oh my world! This has to be the best cookie I have ever tasted," Jeminat, one of the colleagues, said excitedly. "We should get the pastry for the Annual General Meeting (AGM) from the same store."

Nneoma laughed.

"My friend, Osas, here makes them and she doesn't do commercial stuff."

"Are you insane?" Chidinma, the other colleague, screamed in mock alarm. "Listen dear, bake a nice batch for the board meeting we are having next week. If the bosses like your cookies, we can ask you to do same for our AGM and maybe even have some for sale here at breakfast time at the cafeteria!" She continued excitedly.

"This Nneoma, you no be better person o. So, you have just been eating these cookies alone since?" Jeminat teased and all three laughed.

Osas had not said a word since they decided to turn her little cookie into a big business. She knew her cookies were exceptional but she had never thought about going commercial with it. It was beginning to sound exciting and she finally found her voice.

"This sounds good really. Do I have to see anyone to discuss this further?" She asked nervously.
"Chidinma is the madam in charge. She is the head of all things Admin here. If she says bake, you had better bake," Jeminat joked.

"Oh that's great," Osas quipped. "How many people are we baking for? You have seen the cookies, how many do you think will suffice for the board meeting?"

They held a brief talk, discussing numbers. Osas promised to send a quote for the cookies the next day. Nneoma teased Osas about a commission when the business became a household name.

Osas got home at 2:30pm as she had hoped but did not turn on the TV at all. She figured the Telenovela stars were making their money and it was about time she started making hers. It was so exciting thinking of herself a business woman. She could already

112

imagine herself baking cookies with her many staff supplying supermarkets and other chains of stores.

She would call the pastry business Cookies R' Us or Just Cookies.

She decided if she got the AGM gig, and possibly had to place cookies in the cafeteria of such a big office complex, she would need to have a business name, nice labels and a whole lot in place. She knew she had to slow down and take this whole thing one step at a time. She needed to email the quote to Chidinma. The quote was ready in an hour but she wanted to seem cool and not too eager, so she decided to send it the next morning.

Chidi called. She thought about her aunties and took the call. He wasn't a bad guy. Maybe she was being a little too picky, she thought. He promised to pick her up at 7:30pm. That meant she couldn't go jogging in the evening either. Well, she was going to be a business woman soon and she needed to enjoy these lazy times. She laughed at the thought. She dreamt of being a cookie mogul. It was getting exciting.

Chidi picked her up promptly and they had dinner at Casa Lydia in Ikoyi. She was so excited that she spent the entire date talking about the business. Chidi found it amusing, as he had never seen her that animated. He encouraged her to register a business name if she had the deal.

"Any pick on a business name yet?" He asked, keying in to her excitement.

The food was good and the wine excellent but neither cared.

"I was thinking of Just Cookies," Osas said.

113

She loved the enthusiasm he was showing. It was actually endearing.

"Hmmm, sounds catchy but a bit limiting. You did say you make great muffins too, right?" He asked.

Osas nodded at his question. He was making sense. Just Cookies was saying all she made was cookies. So the muffins or any other pastry would seem out of place.

"I guess I have to come up with something more creative and apt," she furrowed her brow.

"You don't have to come up with a name immediately," he teased. "We can at least have dessert; and to show you that I believe in this pastry world business, I will be responsible for everything, registration and all."

Like someone with an epiphany, Osas' face light up.

"That's it!" She shrieked.

"I haven't even finished making the grand proclamation," Chidi joked.

"Pastry World! I love it," she said. "I have a fantasy pastry image in my head where kids can get lost in cookie jars and cookie towers."

"Okay, I wasn't gunning for a name but I guess now more than ever, I am involved as an emotional partner."

They both laughed. It was so much fun talking about it to Chidi. He was interested, supportive and helpful.

Mental note: call Esohe to give her the business gist and the Chidi update.

"Well, back to what I was going to say before you had an epiphany. I will be responsible for all financial costs in creating a webpage and registering the business," he proclaimed dramatically.

Osas was so excited. She thanked him in her own dramatic way.

"I would like to thank my friend, Chidi, who believed in me without even tasting my cookies. I dedicate this pastry award to him."

Was it the wine or her excitement was simply infectious? They were both laughing so hard that other diners stared at them but they were having a great time. Nothing else mattered.

Next morning, she sent the mail to Chidinma and almost immediately she responded and asked if she could add a few muffins to the order. Osas sent another quote and waited. Chidinma responded with a mail asking for her account details and they were in business.

Osas bought all she needed but knew she would need someone to assist her if she was going to have all baked and delivered by 8am for the board meeting. So, she asked her neighbour's daughter for some assistance. She was nervous. She prayed that nothing should go wrong. She could bake the muffins and cookies with her eyes closed but still she couldn't stifle the trepidation.

She arrived Nneoma's office with the cookies and muffins at seven forty-five. Fifteen minutes earlier than the scheduled time. Chidinma was pleased. She loved everything. She promised to stay in touch.

"I am sure they will love the home-baked pastry," she said confidently. "Our CEO, Mr. Guillaume, loves cookies. You know all these oyinbo people na. If he gives his seal of approval, then I can guarantee your pastry a spot in the cafeteria." Osas was overwhelmed.

"I am not trying to bribe you, Chidinma but if I get that opportunity to have my pastry at your cafetaria, then you are guaranteed a lifetime supply of cookies."

She gave her a hug, thanked her and walked towards the elevator. She was whistling in her head, wanted to do a jig but figured she would do that in the elevator. Her first gig! She felt like she had to telepathically send Mr. Guillaume a Like my pastry? memo.

She wanted to call Chidi to give him the good news. They talked more frequently now. He even called to wake her up on time to start baking, though he didn't have to because she was up already. Though they were not dating officially yet, she knew it was just a matter of time unless he did something stupid. She decided she would invite him over for dinner. It would be her way of saying thank you for his support.

She recollected that he spoke about missing his mum's Oha soup playfully a few days ago when he told her he was having noodles for dinner. She could make Oha soup. It would be too heavy for dinner. She would prepare it and hand it over to him to take

116

home. They could have her special peppered snail, vegetable and white rice for dinner. That was not too much for someone who she might be dating soon, and who had also willingly to supported her business. She decided to invite him during a chat via the social media.

Osas: Dinner at my place, you game?

Chidi: Na wa o! No time for plenty talks. Just straight to business!

Osas: Lol. Sorry jare. How you doing?

Chidi: Busy but not too busy for dinner with a gorgeous business woman.

Osas: Lol

Chidi: What time?

Osas: 7pm

Chidi: Can we do 7:30? I have to leave my office at about 6pm.

Osas: No wahala, see you at 7:30

Chidi: Can't wait!

She enjoyed cooking. So, it was really no bother. She had some snails her grandmum sent from Benin. They were so expensive in Lagos! Her grandmum always supplied her garri, plantain, snails and crayfish. Iye was always a lifesaver. She would collect money from Osas' parents to get foodstuff to send to her. She had been doing that since her days in the boarding house in secondary school when she got her provisions. She then moved on to foodstuffs during her days at the university. Now, even as a grown-up and one that was gainfully employed, Iye still did same. Her argument was that that was the least her parents could do for abandoning her. Osas could not agree less with her.

She got into the kitchen to make dinner first. She decided she would prepare the oha afterwards.

Chidi arrived at about twenty minutes past seven. He still had on his work clothes but had taken off the tie and his jacket. He looked every inch a successful investment banker or a model for an investment banking ad.

"Hey gorgeous," he greeted her with a hug and a peck on the cheek, as she opened the door.

She loved his perfume. It was all male and at same time it smelt sweet.

"Hi ya!" She responded. "I hope you came with a big appetite?"

He patted his abs.

"See how flat it is? I have been starving myself all day in preparation for your dinner."

"Yeah, right! Tell that to the gym. Don't blame me for your six packs." She laughed.

"But really, Osas, I am hungry o. Ikeja traffic is enough to do that to anyone."

She took that as her cue and dished his meal and brought it in a tray to him. Her nice little apartment did not have a dining area, so the tray and a stool were suffice.

"Oh my! It looks so good I don't know if I should eat or take a picture of the meal," Chidi teased.

She served herself a small portion and they ate in silence for a while with the TV on though neither of them was watching.

"Osas, this tastes even better than it looks! She bakes, she cooks, she is always pleasant, she is beautiful... the list is simply endless," he admired at her. "You are simply perfect," he added lovingly.

After that comment, nothing was said between them. Just an awkward silence, which Osas had to break.

"Guess what? I have another gig already! Chidinma, the Admin lady, said one of the directors wants me to bake cookies and muffins for fifty people. It's his kid's birthday next weekend and he loves the cookies."

"Wow! That's great!" He said swallowing a little too fast. "You need to get your business registered so people can take your business a lot more seriously. Design a simple invoice and receipt online. I will ask someone to contact you to discuss the business name registration. Let's start with the business cards, which doubles as handbills, then open a bank account in your business name asap!"

She was getting all excited again. So was he too. They talked and planned a bit more. She sensed he was tired, as he kept yawning. She felt selfish keeping him and making him think for her after a hard day but felt grateful, for his inputs were amazing. He was willing to help and it was nice to have let him, she thought.

It was quarter past ten when Chidi stood up to leave.

"I am so tired. I am having a very early start tomorrow," he said.

"Thanks for everything, Chidi, especially for believing in me."

"Things we do for those we care about," he said with a meaningful look.

Osas did not want to see the meaning in his gaze. She quickly excused herself to get his oha. She always ran away. She didn't know why but she just kept running and she wondered if he would stop chasing at some point.

"I made oha," she said when she returned with the plastic bowl. "It may not taste as good as your mum's but it was made with a lot of care too," she said, daring him to say something with her look.

He said nothing, took the bowl from her, set it on the sofa and pulled her close. He said nothing as he looked at her. It was his turn to dare her. He dared her to pull away from his embrace. But she did not. Then, he kissed her. She wasn't sure how long it was but she knew she didn't want it to stop when it did.

"Thank you for dinner," he whispered.

She couldn't find her voice, so she nodded.

He picked up the bowl from the sofa and she saw him off to his car.

The night was going to be a long one. She would spend it talking to Esohe. She would spend it thinking about the kiss and mentally berating herself for taking forever to decide if she wanted to be with Chidi. She could hear Adele's Hello on the radio. She knew she did not want to sing that song.

As promised, Chidi assisted her with the registration of Pastry World as a business name. He went a step further to ask his account officer to hasten her account opening process. In his word: "You must look serious for people to take you seriously." He had told her people should only pay to her business account and not her personal account.

She got the party gig money paid to the new account number, as Chidi made sure everything was done speedily. It felt good seeing the documents from the CAC, then eventually her corporate account cheque book. Everything was happening so fast. He told her to send an official proposal for the AGM and the cafeteria pastry supply to Chidinma. Chidinma was impressed.

"You mean this business o. I am impressed by your tenacity. Your prices are good and you have made it so official too. It would be easy for anyone to actually keep a proper record of all transactions," Chidinma said, as she read through the proposal that Chidi had helped her edit.

"I will do all I can to see that both deals pull through."

Everything was going well. It was two weeks to Christmas and Esohe's wedding. She had accepted her newfound status as a business woman. The AGM and the cafeteria contracts were both approved without a hitch! She had also accepted Chidi into her life. Even her ex-witch of a landlady respected Chidi who was from same state as hers, and now called her my in-law. Chidi was turning out to be her knight in shining armour.

Just about a month ago, she was dreading going to Benin for Christmas. But now, she was looking forward to it. She was a business woman, with a gorgeous and supportive man in her life, who was even ready to make the trip to Benin with her just to meet Iye and Esohe, both people he knew meant the world to her.

She wondered what her aunties would think of Chidi. Probably, they would tell her she made a good catch.

Maybe she did not hate spending Christmas in Benin after all. She just didn't have the right financial, emotional and physical accessories.

She sent Chidi a chat message. She knew he had waited to hear her say it:

Osas: I love you.

In a Gilded Cage

As usual, there is a great woman behind every idiot.

— *John Lennon*

He whistled and bobbed his head to Phyno's Connect as he drove down the highway. He did not understand the language but from the smattering of English in the song, he could tell it was a grass-to-grace story. The song was so apt! Finally, he was moving to Maitama where he really belonged.

He fiddled with the radio and stopped at 88.9 Brila FM. It was his favourite radio station. He loved sports and thought all men should only listen to Brila because it still had that old-school-sport-styled presentation that he grew up with and the music was good too. Music, news and sports were all any real man should listen to on the radio, he mused.

Osezua thought briefly about Chioma, the girl he just left sobbing in her apartment. He felt sorry for her. She had been there for him while he searched for the real deal but now it was time to move on. His plan was to leave her a note and just disappear when she left for the bank where she worked. How was he supposed to know she would come back home complaining of cramp and find him putting the rest of his stuff in his Samsonite case? The case was one of the few acquisitions he had made to give himself the image of a young successful businessman.

"Osezua, why are you doing this?" She asked, perplexed. "I do not deserve this after everything I have done to help you..." she started.

"Listen Chioma, I have expressed my gratitude in more ways than one," he interrupted her. "Besides, you are Igbo and I am Ishan. My family will not allow this to go as far as we would both like."

He wondered why all women seemed to think they helped in some great way. They wanted a tall, dark and handsome guy to hang out with them. They always wanted to impress their friends by how handsome, romantic and polished he was. You would think they would know that all good things come to an end eventually but they were all the same; always whining about how they helped him to find his feet.

"I didn't think it would end this soon but you started talking marriage and I am a man. I cannot completely depend on you. So, I need to sort myself out," he tried to explain but Chioma looked unconvinced.

This must have upset her even more as she became hysterical and started crying.

"You are a fool, Osezua! A big fool and an ingrate," she shrieked. "So, you just discovered your manhood after I have housed you for seven months, fed you and taken care of every sordid and perverse whim of yours?" She screamed. "Suddenly you remember your male pride and family?" She asked rhetorically.

"Chi, I know it's that time of the month, so you are probably more emotional than this actually warrants."

He knew he had put his foot in his mouth by saying that, as her eyes darted to and fro in search of something to throw at him. He felt threatened by the crazed look in her eyes and quickly rolled the suitcase out of her apartment amidst curses that he would die a miserable death and he would suffer for his heartless betrayal. He was cocksure any sense of guilt would evaporate the minute he stepped into the lovely duplex in Maitama that Hajia had set up for him.

Osezua used to be a banker in Lagos before moving to Abuja and meeting Chioma, then Hajia. But somewhere along the line, the bank had to downsize and there he was, fine boy without a job. It was at that moment of despair that he met Deji.

Deji was one of the customers at the bank Osezua worked. He always deposited money but no one was sure if he had any reasonable particular source of income. Neither was there a trace to any meaningful business. Osezua and his colleagues assumed he was one of those cybercriminals.

After losing his job, he ran into Deji somewhere in Surulere. Looking as suave and well dressed as always. He offered to buy him lunch after Osezua told him of his recent jobless state. After lunch and a few drinks, he offered to introduce the very broke and desperate Osezua to his business. Deji was a gigolo!

He mentioned a few society women in Lagos and Abuja that he had done business with. Most of them married and with more money than they knew what to do with. He explained how being a boy-toy was the in-thing and he had so much money to show for it.

"Listen bro, it's nothing," he said calmly. "They require a particular service and I provide it." He explained like a true salesman: "I wasn't going to mention it but you complained about your rent here in Surulere. Just five hundred thousand and you have been out of a job for a few months. How do you intend paying?" He mocked. "I can easily give you the cash but when will you pay back? I don't believe in giving someone handouts. I subscribe to the cliché that you don't give a man a fish but you teach him how to fish," Deji said matter-of-factly.

"Guy, these are old women na. Most of them probably old enough to be my mum," Osezua said with distaste.

"How old are you?" He asked.

"Twenty eight," was the response.

"Then be a man and stop talking like a child. You are tall, goodlooking and there is a very ready client," he said. "She can pay this your rent or get you an apartment in Lekki this week if she likes you."

He talked about how much he had made, how many trips he had made to several countries while Osezua listened to the benefits with keen interest and in awe of how easy this could be.

A few days later, Osezua was introduced to the client.

All this was two years ago in Lagos. His first client had been very straightforward. She had almost made it sound like it was a real business deal. She needed him around for three months. For her, it was payback for the years she had coped with her husband's infidelity.

She rented an apartment for him in Lekki. He accompanied her on a business trip to Turkey. She flew first class; he flew economy and they met back at the hotel. He was supposedly her assistant on the trip.

He made a few hundred thousand Naira, got a decent wardrobe in those three months and he was hooked.

He always consulted Deji when in a fix. Deji was his egbon in the newfound line of work. He realized soon enough that you had to be a gigolo and sometimes a con artist.

He dated several rich older ladies but none wanted him for keeps. Osezua wanted one that would invest in him enough for him to be rid of them completely but that hadn't happened for him yet. He admired Deji who had been with the same older woman for years now. Everyone knew about them and she was a widow with more money than she knew what to do with. Deji was set for life. Osezua wanted same and till he found the real deal he would settle for the in-betweens. Osezua had since discovered that the right targets could be found if you strategized.

With the older women who wanted a boy toy, Osezua didn't have to pretend. Each knew what they wanted out of the partnership. But with the middle-aged ladies with money and desperately in search of a husband or baby-daddy, he had to play the conman. His last client in Lagos was Mfon. He winced as he thought of her and how she practically ran him out of Lagos. She had made Lagos inhabitable for him. He had no choice but to relocate for fear of what she could do to him.

 Mfon was in her early forties, a manager in one of the oil servicing companies. She had bought a house in one of those gated estates close to Chevy Drive in Lekki. He started seeing her under the pretext of being a contractor with a government parastatal. People like Mfon did not become successful without a bit of shrewdness and intelligence. Mfon knew Osezua was full of hot air when he talked about his projects but she wanted to get married and was ready to put up with his rubbish as long as he knew she was the boss.

He borrowed money from her to complete the imagined projects he was working on, showed her several false documents to support his claim and it went on for a few months. She put up with Osezua's shenanigans until the day she found out he was seeing Mrs. Tongo, the senator whom she had introduced to him. He even went on a trip with the senator to Abu Dhabi after asking she, Mfon, had given him money to go to Uromi to see his supposed sick mother. She confronted him when he returned from the trip. Without batting an eye, he told her he was through with her.

"Listen Mfon, your suspicions are getting ridiculous," he said trying to keep a straight face as he denied the accusations. "Maybe we should take a break till you cool off," he said nonchalantly.

He was tired and wanted to end the relationship. The senator was more promising, generous and never nagged. He forgot the saying that hell hath no fury like a woman scorned.

Mfon made Osezua's life a living hell in Lagos. She ruined him socially. Had people spread rumours about him. Popular blogs featured unfounded stories about him. She also sent thugs to his house to roughen him up. On one occasion, she had him set up for rape and he spent a few days in prison.

When he was eventually let out of prison, he went to plead with Mfon to let him be. Her condition speeded his exile to Abuja.

"I don't want to mistakenly see you anywhere on the Island or hanging out with people I know," she had threatened. "If I see you, I will come up with new ways to make your life a living hell," she added without emotion. "Osezua, this Lagos is not big enough for both of us," she told him coldly. "You have duped me several times, I did not mind. You made moves on my cousin, I turned a blind eye," she listed my offences, ticking them off on her well-manicured nails. "Then you travelled with the senator, my god-mother and you come back to insult my intelligence with your lies. If you know what is good for you, you will move to Ikorodu or Badagry immediately. Places I will never bump into your stupid face ever or else…" She was ominous and livid with anger.

He spoke with Deji and a few friends and they decided there was really nothing keeping him in Lagos, so he moved to Abuja. He stayed in a decent hotel somewhere in Wuse for a short while, had lunch at the Hilton and a few choice places looking for easy targets but it did not happen as fast as he thought. Then he met Chioma, who took the pressure of hustling off him for the meantime.

It was not difficult to come up with a story after a month at the hotel as to how the deal that brought him to Abuja was not completely sealed. He moved to a friend's place in Garki when he became short of cash.
He knew he had to think fast as the friend's place he was staying for a short while was no longer convenient. The chap was getting married.

Chioma, twenty-nine and desperate for marriage, acted like an ageing spinster. Osezua still had his beat-up car from Lagos, still had his charm and Chioma did not see through his deceptive acts. The move to her place was meant to be temporary till he closed a deal he was working on. If only she knew the deal he meant would leave her feeling hurt, betrayed and used!

She felt excited taking care of him, and was sure when he made some real money he would marry her.

Well, it took him 5 months to close the supposed deal. That was how long it took him to find Hajia.

He met Hajia on a day he wasn't even hunting. Osezua had gone to the hospital to visit a friend who had undergone a major surgery when he saw her alight from a chauffeur-driven, hunter green BMW. She looked like she was made of money. Regal was the only word he could think of. She was light-skinned, with an effervescence that was peculiar to some North-Eastern Nigerians.

He wondered if he could ever have a shot at someone like her. She was draped in diamonds and looked stunning for a woman her age. He stole another glance at her. Their eyes met and he quickly averted his but not before seeing her smirk.

Damn! He had messed this up, he thought. He should have kept his gaze locked and not let her think of him being intimidated. He turned around to redeem himself but she had walked away.

He returned to the reception a few minutes later to make a call when he saw her again. She was looking intently at a documentary on contemporary art and he knew this was his chance.

He dug into his inner Barry-White voice and asked: "Are you a collector?"

"Are you an artist?" She asked without turning around.

He sensed she knew it was him. Her perfume was making him heady, sensual and all feminine.

"No," he said. "Just a young man with a penchant for all things exquisite," he added suggestively.

131

She turned around, her eyes as cold as steel. Up-close, she was even more stunning and breathtaking. She reminded Osezua of one of the senators from his state. He willed himself not to look away. He held her gaze this time and she smiled. A smile that did not quite get to her eyes but that which did not diminish her aura either.

"Are you obedient?" She asked pointedly.

"Depends on who is instructing?" he replied.

"I'll be," she said, scrutinizing him unabashedly. "So, are you obedient?" she asked again.

Osezua looked at her and said, "I am loyal and…"
She cut him mid-sentence. "I have a Daschund. Its name is Yoshi. Yoshi is loyal but not very obedient. Two different virtues Mr.…?" She waited for him to complete it.

"Osezua Omijie," he added quickly. He was not thrilled at the comparison with her dog but she didn't seem like one who should be kept waiting.

She whipped out a business card from a cold caseholder. He reached for it and she held it back for a second.

"Write your number behind my card. I will call you if I have a reason to."

He did as she instructed. She walked away without leaving her name. He hoped she would call. He also wanted her to respect him a little, so he did not ask either.

132

She called him a week later.

"So, Osezua Omijie, loyalty or obedience?" she asked the minute he said 'hello'.

"Who is this?" he feigned ignorance, hoping that she did not hang up the phone.
"Meet me at Chop Sticks at 9pm. You do know where that is?" She asked as though he wasn't expected to know it.

"I know they make a crisp and tasty breaded prawn," he said.

"A simple yes would have sufficed," she said. "Don't keep me waiting."

He wondered what kind of relationship theirs would be. She sounded like a dominatrix.

Their relationship was a bit difficult for Osezua from the start. She was generous but at same time, she ordered him around like a help. She had got him a nice apartment in Maitama. He suspected it was one of her property. She was very private and said nothing about her personal life. It was rumoured that she was a concubine of an ex-president. She had a son residing in Canada and more money and property than Osezua could wrap his little mind around.

She had taken him on a trip to Spain and then to Germany on business trips. She referred to him constantly as her employee; this he detested considering their relationship. She rang him one morning to say that her driver, Yusuf, was ill and that he should come drive her to a meeting.

He arrived at her mansion in Asokoro as instructed. She made him drive her to a few meetings in a brand new Toyota Camry. New, but still not exotic like her other cars, he reckoned. It must have been a gift from one of her contractors because she would not buy a Camry for her own use ordinarily. He was instructed to wait in the car like a common driver.

Osezua boiled from within throughout the outing but kept his cool. He gave her curt responses when asked any question and even addressed her as Madam a few times. She ignored his sarcasm and seemed amused by his sulkiness.

He dropped her off when she was done and asked coldly, "Should I leave the keys at the gate with the security man or bring it inside?"

"Why would you want to leave your keys with the security man?" She asked mischievously with a glint in her eyes.

Osezua was confused. Then it dawned on him: the car was his!

"Yes, the car is yours. Why would I want a Camry in my garage?" she asked, still amused by the shocked look on his face.
"You can give that rickety thing you drive a break. I am sick of hearing your tale of endless confrontations with your mechanic," she added.

"I am still in shock!" Osezua gushed. "I don't know what to say," he babbled.

"Just be good and obedient and you won't have to worry about money."

She sounded like the devil asking him for his soul but he didn't care. He had a brand new car. This gig was finally beginning to pay real money.

"Thank you so much, Hajia. Wow! A brand new car!' He screamed. "You will be spending the night here. I am sure you can come up with ways to say thank you," she said walking away.

Osezua wanted to call his family but he always felt embarrassed, as he never quite knew how to explain how he got a new car or how he had been making the trips. He had told his family that he was in business with some friends and that things were slow. He did not have enough cash to justify his newfound lifestyle. He called Deji instead.
"D for Deji!" He hailed. "Egbon, Hajia is just spoiling me anyhow o," he said. "Your guy has just been given a brand new Camry as we speak."

"Nice one! That's how it should be. You have put in almost three years in this gig, you should be cashing in seriously," Deji congratulated him. "Just be careful with her o! She is not one to mess with. I know her clique very well," he warned.

They spoke for a few more minutes before he joined Hajia in the main building.

Osezua understood clearly for the first time that he was no longer in control of his life one Saturday evening while sitting with Hajia on the foyer. He had received a call from his younger sister saying she had to come to Abuja for an interview and naturally she assumed she would stay at his apartment. He mentioned it casually to Hajia, who rected angrily. Her reaction was unexpected.

135

"This is not your family house, Osezua. She cannot stay here," she said sternly.

"But sweetheart, it's just three days. She will be gone after the interview," he pleaded.

"She cannot stay here, Osezua. And do not call me Sweetheart. I find it disrespectful," she said calmly and stood up to wear her slip on. "Ask Yusuf to wait for me in the car while I freshen up," she said, dismissing the subject completely.

He had to lie to his sister that he was not in town and the house was locked. He had to deal with several embarrassing situations like this from Hajia. She had once seized his car keys in Area 10 when she saw him drop off an old classmate who happened to be female. They had both had lunch at Mama Cass and he dropped her off. Hajia had seen and trailed them from the restaurant to point he dropped her. As she was about to alight, he gave her a friendly hug and waved. Then he saw Hajia's car parked in front of his. Yusuf came down and walked up to his side of the car.

"Madam say make I collect the car key," he said sombrely.

"Excuse me, what do you mean by that?" Osezua asked nervously.

"Oga, she say make I bring the key," Yusuf repeated.

"Ose, what's going on?" his passenger asked, a bit worried by the commotion.
"It's just a misunderstanding with my boss. It's nothing really," he stuttered in embarrassment. "Don't worry, it will be sorted out. You take care. We will talk later."

He got out of the car and walked to the SUV parked in front of him. They were beginning to attract the attention of onlookers.

"Hajia, what's the meaning of this?" he asked in an almost pleading tone. "Nneka is an old classmate I bumped into and we just had lunch."

"Osezua, hand the keys over to Yusuf."

Osezua tried one last time to reason with her. "Please Hajia, this is really embarrassing. We don't have to leave the car on the road here. Let me take it to Asokoro while we discuss this," he was really desperate and just needed to leave the scene.

She thought about it for a second and reckoned there was no point leaving the car unattended to in Garki.

"I will see you in Asokoro," she said and beckoned on Yusuf to get in the car.

As they drove off, Osezua walked to his car quickly, still a bit shaken. He had put up with a lot from Hajia in the past six months and it wasn't getting any better. He had the money and all the trapping. Yeah! Trappings. That was what they were. He could barely travel unless Hajia permitted it. She had compared him to her Daschund when they first met, but evidently, the Daschund was treated with a lot more care and respect.

He could barely remember what it was like to be in control of his own time and money. He longed for a normal relationship with a woman he loved and who loved him. He had been in this path for the past three years, and he wondered if being a gigolo was worth it.

He drove quietly towards the house in Asokoro. He knew he had to be his own man and do something but he remembered what it was like without a job and how easy it was to just live in a lovely mansion, shop, wear good clothes, go on vacation and just tolerate a spoilt rich older woman. He compared both lives and he knew he was raised better than this but he was not going to give up on all this, at least not yet.

He took a good look at Hajia's mansion as he drove in. This was the life he had always wanted, and this was the life he deserved. Comfort and its trappings were certainly trumping his conscience and freedom. He was not turning his back on all this. Maybe in a few years' time, he thought.

The Passenger

Dealing with people is probably the biggest problem you face, especially if you are in business. Yes, and that is also true if you are a housewife, architect or engineer.

- Dale Carnegie

"Oga Driver, abeg na, make you pass Ajao side go Airport. I am running late," I said to the driver after two hours in traffic.

There had been an accident on the Third Mainland Bridge and I was nowhere near the airport for my flight to Benin. I had been trying to secure an appointment with the Minister of Works and Housing for close to three months and I had just found out from a reliable source that he was attending the wedding of an Edo State dignitary's daughter, Obehi. Obehi and I had been good friends from our days in the university in England, so I had an invite.

It was Saturday, the wedding day and I was not going to miss it for anything. I had a well-crafted plan nicely thought out and I was going to give the minister an elevator pitch. Thirty seconds' talk that would leave him longing for more information. Then I would strike. The Minister of Works and Housing was known for his ingenious ideas and out-of-the-box approach to tackling problems. I was sure my ideas on affordable housing would impress him if only I could get him to hear them.

I was all set in my grey Kaftan, my Ipad and an overnight pilot bag. I knew I would need to spend the night in Benin and, at least, party with Obehi and her husband. Though that was secondary. My mission was meeting the minister, Dr. Raji Tongo.

140

I looked at my watch again. It was 11:30am. My flight was originally a 12-noon flight but the airline had called to reschedule. The flight was now for 1:30pm. This they did at 9am when I had already checked in online and headed for the airport. I had cursed and

sworn at them for a while but now I was grateful they did as there was no way I would have made it to the airport for 12 noon.

Fifteen minutes later we were on the same spot just descending the Third Mainland Bridge and I knew Mobolaji Bank Anthony was an unreliable route to take. It would always be traffic-jammed at this time on a Saturday. The fuel stations at the roundabout were always the major cause of the traffic. The Catholic Church at the turn to Mende also would most likely have a wedding going on.

So I emphasized again, "Driver, please take Oshodi and enter through Ajao."

"Oga, I no deaf na. I hear you the first time," the driver said, irritated by my harassment. He muttered inaudibly under his breath.

The day had started off badly. I woke up a bit later than I wanted to. My flatmate was supposed to take me to the airport from our apartment in the estate before VGC but that was not to be, as his car failed to start. After several troubleshooting attempts, I quickly resorted to calling a car hire company. While two of them said the time was too short and there was no available vehicle, I found a winner with the third and I quickly showered and waited.

It was almost 9am and the cab was meant to pick me up at 8:45, so I called the company again.

"Hello, my name is Onaivi. I booked a cab earlier," I stated. "I am still waiting for it even though it was meant to be here at 8:45am."

The lady on the other end answered in a very bored tone. "It's just 9:55 na, be patient. I am sure the driver is on his way," she said nonchalantly. "You know Ajah is far, if you were in Victoria Island or Lekki, it would be easier," she succinctly reminded me that it was my fault for not living in the better part of the Island.

I was about to say something rude or explain that the Chevron Roundabout was not part of Ajah but thought of a better response. So, instead I asked: "Please, can I have the driver's number so I know where he is?"

She gave his name and number and hung up immediately. Poor service was the least of my worries at that point. I just wanted to get to the airport in time. I called the driver. I dialled three times before he finally picked up his phone.

"Hello! Is that Razak?" I asked

"Yes Sir!" he replied.

"My name is Onaivi. I am waiting for you to pick me up. I am going to the airport!"

"Ha! Oga, the go-slow delay me small, because of you I try to take one-way and now, LASTMA don stop me," he explained like I was to blame. "You go look for another vehicle," he said without an apology and hung up.

I was too stunned and was about calling him back when my flatmate, Chuka, brought me to my senses. "Guy, why you wan call am back na?" he asked. "Go take taxi for front of Estate gate jor!"

I quickly grabbed my bag and boarded a roadside cab for the airport. I was already worried at the thought of missing the flight, though I had checked in online and printed my boarding pass. But then, somewhere around the Lekki Toll Gate, I received the airline's text message informing me about the rescheduling and I relaxed.

Funny how they call it a reschedule to avoid passengers saying the flight was delayed. Either way, rescheduled or delayed, I was fine with the new flight schedule.

If the flight took off at 1pm, I would be in Benin at about 1:30 and the cab would take me straight to Ring Road where the reception was holding somewhere around Bishop Kelly. I would still have enough time to see the Minister and party with the couple.

I sat down and browsed through my presentation. Made some bullet points for my short pitch and read through the entire proposal again. I looked up for a bit and saw we were approaching the Third Mainland Bridge. We were making good time till we got closer to the bridge.

I could not see the end of the traffic line, neither could anyone tell what the cause was. Some said the road was blocked for some repairs; others said there had been a robbery or an accident. People just sat down in their cars and in their frustration came up with possible reasons for the traffic. Most were dressed for one event or the other. I was probably one of the few people trying to get to the airport, and most likely the only one trying to pitch to a Minister at a friend's wedding. It was a standstill and I was getting nervous. What if this lasted longer than usual? "What's the cause of this traffic?" I asked rhetorically in frustration but the cab driver responded anyway.

"Oga, na me and you dey here na. How I go take know?"

I beat back a response and watched helplessly. I tried going on twitter to read traffic reports. Probably, someone would be talking about it. There was no data service. There never was on the bridge, I remembered.

At 12:15pm, we were at Oshodi and there was a bit of traffic there as well but after that, it was good. I arrived at the airport at 12:40pm and saw the counter had been closed for check-in.

I was happy I had my boarding pass already and walked to the departure lounge. I saw one of the staff of the airline I was about to fly with and stopped her. She responded to my hello defensively and I sensed trouble.

"The flight to Benin, is it boarding yet?" I asked.

"No,' she responded and was about to walk away.

"Excuse me, when are we boarding? It is meant to take off in fifteen minutes," I said as calmly as I could.

"I don't know, sir. When they start boarding, you will hear the announcement," she said, and attempted to walk away again. "I know you are busy and, but you must have an idea…" I stuttered in frustration.

"Sir, the aircraft scheduled to operate the Benin flight is not even on ground as we speak," she interrupted. "When I have an ETA on the flight, they will announce and we will know when Benin will board." She paused to let it sink in, looked at me like I was really stopping her from doing more important things. This time, I let her walk away.

Every second wasted kept me even farther from the Honourable Minister and I did not like it one bit. It was 1:30pm, I was beginning to sweat in anxiety. I walked to the airline's desk for an update. The staff were chatting away and doing nothing that looked remotely helpful.

"Excuse me, is there an update on the Benin flight?" I asked no one in particular.

"The aircraft is almost here," one of them responded casually. I was livid with anger.

"What do you mean by almost here? Is it a bus in traffic? I don't understand how you can all sit here chatting away after the delays and reschedules on a 12-noon flight!" I yelled my frustration.

"Sir, take it easy. It's just one hour," one of the females in the group said. "Benin is not far. Even international flights experience delays," she said unhelpfully, as though that explanation ought to suffice. This was maddening but I knew further exchange with them would yield nothing. I walked back to the departure lounge. I overheard them talking about how we all complained.

I called a few friends who were already in Benin, and was told the wedding did not kick off as early as scheduled and they were still in church rounding off the photo session with family and friends.

"We are just about heading to the reception venue. It's not far from the church," my friend, Nnamdi, informed me. "I told you we should come in yesterday, attend the traditional marriage ceremony, stay in a hotel and attend the white wedding today," he reminded me.

Yes, Nnamdi had suggested that. In retrospect, I felt I should have done heeded his advice. If I failed to see the Minister, the decision not to arrive Benin a day earlier was one I was going to regret.

It was almost 2pm when the aircraft scheduled for Benin landed. We boarded hurriedly like it was a molue, and then one of the airport staff checking the ticket told me I had to check in my hand luggage or get it tagged that it was too large for the overhead locker of the small aircraft. I gave it to them and was given a tag as we boarded.

We arrived Benin at about 3pm and I waited for my luggage. Being that there was no conveyor belt at the Benin airport, we waited for the luggage to be brought in manually by baggage handlers. Fifteen minutes later, they were done and my bag was nowhere in sight.

"Excuse me, please. I have a claim tag for my luggage but I haven't seen it," I asked one of the handlers. He looked at me suspiciously.

"You sure say you check am in?" he asked.

I was going to say that was a dumb question since I had a claim tag that showed I did but instead I nodded affirmatively.

"Ha! That means say your bag don lost o, bros," he said with a worried look that was the best he could muster. "Go see Airport Manager," he advised.

The Airport Manager was polite but not particularly helpful.

"From what I can see here, Sir, the aircraft boarded same time as a flight to Abuja from Lagos. I suspect it was put on the wrong aircraft by accident," he explained. "We apologise for any inconvenience," he recited like a robot. "If you can just leave us your number, we will call you as soon as we locate your luggage."

I gave him my card and quickly left the airport. I went to the cab rank and the young cheerful cab guy asked if I had any luggage. I felt like telling him about the day from hell and how my luggage had gone missing, but I didn't.

"Bishop Kelly, please," I said in a tired voice.

It was 3:37pm. I had given up on meeting the Honourable Minister. These big men rarely ever stayed till the end of these events. I was still thinking about the stress I had been through when I heard the cab driver say, "Seven thousand Naira." I wasn't sure what he was talking about so I asked, "What did you just say?"

"Sir, I said your fare is seven thousand Naira," he repeated.

At this point, I lost my cool completely.

"You dey mad? Bishop Kelly na five minutes from here. You think say I be mugu? Look my face well o. I be Edo boy!" I reeled out in Pidgin English in a way I had not done in years.

"Bros, take am easy na. I no know say na this one along Airport Road you dey go," he said stupidly.

There was only one Bishop Kelly Centre in Benin and we both knew it. I got out of the vehicle as soon as we arrived at the venue and threw two thousand Naira notes at him. I was tired of having a bad day. I was just going to locate my friends and drink myself silly. I was done trying.

The security at the venue was tight. A lot of prominent guests were in attendance. I presented my invitation card and was ushered in. There were cards on the seats indicating where guests were to be seated according to their invites but I was more interested in faces. Familiar faces, friends I could tell my tale of woes. I decided to go say hello to the couple before finding a place to sit and hit the bottle. I hugged Obehi, shook hands with her husband and apologized for coming late.

Just then I heard a voice behind me.

"Obehi, I am about to leave."

He almost shoved me aside to hug her. How rude, I thought. Age does not give anyone the right to cut in in front of another person. "Uncle, this is the friend I was telling you about," I heard Obehi say. "Oh, young man, I like your ideas; very innovative. Obehi showed me a draft of your proposal as regards IDPs," he said shaking my hands.

They were both looking at me. Then, it dawned on me. The elderly man who had shoved me aside was the Honourable Minister himself!

Before I could find my voice for an elevator pitch, he dug into his wallet, gave me his card and all I heard was: "See me in Abuja next week Tuesday. We should discuss this extensively."

I never got to give an elevator pitch to the Minister but I had an appointment, which was even better.

I looked at Obehi in disbelief. All she did was wink mischievously. I went to the bar. I needed a drink.

The Boy in the Garden

Death ends a life, not a relationship.

- *Mitch Albom*

For my late brother AB, this is how I remember you. This is me telling the world how to remember you.

T he soil is red in Benin.

I recall my elderly uncle in Ughoton once told us it was blood soil. His story, was that there had been many wars fought on Benin soil and the blood of those slain had forever changed the soil. It made little sense to me as a child. Then I visited the East and saw something similar, the earth was red there too. Probably, the Biafra war made their soil red, who was to know?

It was August 10, 1996; a day like any other. The only difference was the sadness in our house. The number of people coming and going. Then there was our garden. No one bothered to water it. No one cared to. It didn't matter anymore. The reddish dust was everywhere. The rains had stopped. August break it was called. It was the day we lost Ehigie.

I remember looking out of the window and wondering if the garden was ever going to look the same again. I wondered if Ehigie had taken with him the lush and beauty of the garden.

Our father had always thought it would be a good idea to have a garden like we had in our old house on Dover Road in Ekpoma. The garden had been the envy of all the neighbours. Daddy had a large expanse of land, an enviable property on Ugbor Road, in the GRA area of Benin. The most outstanding part of this was not the building itself, it was the garden. A breath-taking orchard and a flower garden that could be seen through the very low fence. One would think he was a horticulturist considering how much time and money he invested in the garden.

He was an engineer with one of the oil exploration companies in Lagos. He had moved his family to Benin because he was always off shore and thought it would be a better place for us to grow up, learn the mother-tongue and spend time with other family members. So, we moved to Benin.

Before leaving Lagos, our parents had my older sister, Isi and I, Ebehi. Isibhakhome was Isi's full name name in my local dialect, *Ishan* . It meant I found favour in a strange land. Like most people from my part of the country, names were always meaningful and based on real experiences.

My parents moved to Lagos just after their wedding in Ekpoma. Daddy got a job with Alumaco in the late 70s. A few months after the great job came Isi. According to my parents, Lagos had been good to them on all fronts.

When I was born, they wished for a boy but still celebrated by naming me Ebehireme, which means What God has given.

The move to Benin welcomed my brother. Ehigie was born on the 8th of October. He was the light of our world. Ehigie was light skinned, much lighter than Isi and I. He also had really long lashes which Isi kept complaining was wasted on a boy. He was adorable! Daddy was so happy and proud. He named him Ehigie which means God-sent. We all agreed he was truly god-sent. Happy, cute, charming and full of life t-hat was Ehigie.

He spent a lot of time in the garden when he was two years old. He would chase butterflies, pluck flowers and watch our maiguard water the flowers. He loved to wave at passers-by from our low fence. One of our neighbours had been the first to refer to him as the cute little boy in the garden.

I could not breathe. The constriction in my chest was one I could not explain. I wanted to cry but I could not. Perhaps, it was the shock or was it the sight of Isi and my mum crying over Ehigie's lifeless body that numbed me? I just stood and stared.

"Go and call Brother Alex from the next street," Dad said to no one in particular. Being the only one not crying hysterically, I guessed he was referring to me.

12:07am on the 10th of August, 1996 was the moment we lost Ehigie to cerebral malaria after a six-year battle. Six years of paralysis. Six years of pain. Six years that had drained us mentally, physically and financially.

Mama was worst hit by all these. She had had to stop her small business for the entire six years, travelling from place to place in search of a cure or healing. She went from one recommended hospital to another. She visited several countless doctors, physiotherapists and other medical professionals but got nothing in form of a cure. The hospital became her home for several years.

As I walked to the next street in the dead of the night to call Brother Alex, I heard the Udeivbu's ferocious bulldog barking. Normally, I would be scared. But I was not mentally conscious enough to know fear. The dog probably sensed my anguish and gave up barking.

I thought of Ehi's birthday coming up in two months. He would have been 8 years old on the 8th of October, 1996. Like his last five birthdays, there was going to be no celebration, as he was bedridden. But, for the first time, there would be no celebrant either.

I thought about the stiffness in his joints, the bedsores; those times it seemed he was trying to say something but could only grunt through gritted teeth and those times we would see recognition in his lovely eyes…. I was crying in my head and in my heart but still no tears.

I still could not cry. Was it guilt? That morning, I had read Dad's copy of Fred Bauer's Daily Living, Daily Giving and it had something to say about sick relatives.

"… Lord put your healing hand on the patients and mercifully grant them quick release from pain..!"

So, that morning I had asked God to relieve Ehigie in whatever form necessary, and that same night he died. I knew I did not kill him. I knew he was better off dead than the pain and anguish he was going through, but still…!

This all started one night six years ago when Ehigie woke up screaming. Mum would later tell us he was staring at a particular spot in shock like there was something he saw that got him riled up. He was barely two years old. Being a fervent Christian, mum had prayed and rebuked all seen and unseen forces and took him to the hospital as soon as they noticed his rising temperature and taken ill all of a sudden. A trip to the hospital, several pokes and turns by some inexperienced student doctors as mum watched helplessly, he died or so, we thought.

Dad never talked about Ehigie. All I have was Mum's version. She told us Ehigie stopped breathing and one of the baby doctors had pronounced him dead. When she was already crying and grieving for her dead son, then came the mature doctor who found a pulse. She was happy for a while but the happiness was shortlived. Ehigie could not speak, walk or do anything. He just lay there. He was alive only meant he could breathe and his lovely eyes would stay open when he was awake.

Now, he was gone. To a better place away from the world that did not deserve him.

I got to Uncle Alex's and told him Dad wanted him at the house immediately. He wanted to know why.

"Is everybody okay?" he asked.

"Ehigie is dead," I said bluntly.

He heaved a sigh. It sounded like a sigh of relief and for that brief second, I hated him.

A few minutes later we were in our home. Dad took Ehi from Mum's arm and walked into the room with the lifeless body. They were planning an early morning funeral at the local cemetery.

I finally cried. I could not hold back the tears anymore. I was not wailing like Mum or Isi. I could taste the salt in my tears. That was how I knew I was crying. I felt I was going to pass out from the pain in my head and in my heart.

I went over to console my mum. I knew then that Ehigie would not walk our gardens ever again.

Acknowledgements

Osose Aziba, Alexander Sho-Silva, for those hours put into this. Thank you so much.

Onayimi Ani, Nandir Taupyen, Leye Makanjuola, Evelyn Boardman, Uzoamaka Nwakaji, your friendship and support came at different stages in my life. This is me telling the world, I love you guys!

The Amos and Mabel Aigiomawu Family, I would choose you all over and over again.

My little sister and biggest literary ally, Obehi Aigiomawu, I see you.

Editor's Note

The story, "Diary of a Wedding Planner," was first featured in its unedited form in *The Sun* newspaper in 2010.

Printed in Great
Britain
by Amazon